SPACESHIP SALVAGE

By

Ryan Michael Upton

Table of Contents

COPYRIGHT PAGE

SPACESHIP SALVAGE

ISBN 978-1-7646227-3-8 Paperback

First published in Australia in 2026.

Kindle Edition.

Cover design and illustrations by the author.

CHAPTER ONE

THE SHAPE OF FEAR

Ryan almost let go of the tether.

The thought came without warning, sharp and complete, as if it had always been there, waiting for the moment he stopped paying attention.

His fingers tightened instead.

The line held. Thin. Tensioned. Real.

It was the only thing that was.

Everything else fell away.

As if there were no barrier between him and anything, no protection except what he carried on his back and wore against his skin. The suit pressed around him, firm in places, uncomfortably loose in others, a manufactured boundary that made promises it could not guarantee.

His breathing sounded too loud.

Each inhale scraped through the helmet speakers, too close to his ears, too present. It filled the space where everything else should have been. There was no wind. No distant noise. No movement that didn't come from him.

Only the sound of staying alive.

He focused on his hand.

It drifted in front of him, slower than it should have, the motion lagging behind intention. The suit resisted, then followed, as if translating his decisions through something thicker than air. His fingers spread. Closed. Spread again.

A tremor ran through them.

He tried to still it.

It didn't stop.

Fear didn't spike. It didn't surge or overwhelm. It settled.

Heavy. Patient.

It sat behind his ribs and worked its way outward, slowing him down, forcing each movement through resistance that wasn't physical but felt just as real. It didn't tell him to panic. It told him to hesitate.

And hesitation, out here, was its own kind of danger.

Ryan swallowed, the motion amplified inside the helmet, louder than it should have been.

He forced his gaze outward.

There was no direction to look.

The stars surrounded him completely, packed into the darkness with a precision that erased depth. They didn't feel distant. They felt fixed, as if he had been placed inside them rather than beneath them.

No horizon.

No up.

No reference point his body could trust.

His stomach tightened, expecting gravity to correct the mistake, to pull him into alignment with something that made sense.

It didn't.

It never did.

Afraid of space.

The words formed cleanly, without resistance.

He didn't argue with them.

It sounded simple when phrased that way. Almost childish. But there was nothing simple about this. This wasn't fear of darkness. It wasn't fear of height.

It was the fear of absence.

No ground.

No air.

No forgiveness.

He had felt versions of it before. Standing too close to an edge. Looking up into the open sky that seemed too large to belong to anything real. Moments where the world felt wider than it should have been, where the limits he depended on blurred just enough to make him aware they existed at all.

Space removed those limits entirely.

It didn't stretch them.

It erased them.

His grip tightened again on the tether, the line pressing into his glove just enough to remind him it was there. A connection. A constraint. Something that defined distance in a place that rejected measurement.

He checked it without meaning to.

Then again.

Still secure.

That helped. He exhaled slowly, watching a faint trace of condensation bloom against the inside of his visor before fading just as quickly.

Why this? The question surfaced with the same quiet persistence as the fear itself.

Why choose this?

Of all the directions his life could have taken, of all the systems he could have stayed inside, controlled, structured, predictable, why step into the one place that stripped all of that away?

The answer didn't arrive cleanly.

It never did.

Because fear had edges.

It defined where he stopped.

And at some point, those edges had become too small.

Staying inside systems that failed in quieter ways had started to feel worse than facing one that failed all at once.

He flexed his hand again.

The tremor was still there.

Smaller.

Controllable.

That was enough.

A salvage job.

The words felt mechanical compared to everything around him. Simple. Procedural. Approach. Assess. Retrieve. Systems he understood. Problems that could be broken down and solved.

That part made sense.

He felt nervous as his gaze drifted back into the open black, into the depth that refused to resolve into anything his mind could process.

Instinct told him to stop.

To hold a position.

To not move any farther away from anything solid than he already was.

He ignored it.

Slowly, deliberately, he reached forward along the tether.

Pulled.

His body followed, drifting through the void in a controlled line, movement translated through tension and restraint rather than direction or force.

The fear didn’t leave.

It adjusted.

Shifted into something that could exist alongside motion instead of preventing it.

He pulled again.

Closer.

Still attached.

Out here, that was the only measure that mattered.

And for now, he was holding onto it.

CHAPTER TWO

THE PRICE OF SILENCE

The tether pulled tighter.

Ryan felt it before he saw it, a subtle change in tension that travelled through his glove and into his arm, a shift.

He stopped moving.

The line angled slightly now, no longer a straight path back to Bessy but a shallow curve, drifting under forces too small to notice until they accumulated into something real.

He followed it with his eyes.

For a moment, nothing made sense.

Then he saw it.

A fragment passed in the distance, dark against darker, moving fast enough that his eyes struggled to track it. Small. Irregular. It didn't glow. Didn't reflect. It simply crossed his field of vision.

His nerves returned.

Debris.

The word landed cleanly.

He scanned again, slower this time, forcing his breathing to steady. The stars didn't help. They never did. Too many fixed points, too much noise for the eye to filter properly.

Then another shift.

Physical.

The tether vibrated faintly, a barely perceptible tremor that ran along its length.

Something had passed closer this time.

Ryan held still, resisting the instinct to pull himself back too quickly. Sudden movement out here was its own problem. Momentum didn't forgive mistakes. It multiplied them.

He waited.

Counted his breathing.

One.

Two.

Three.

Nothing else crossed his vision.

The tension in the tether settled.

Stable.

That was enough.

For now.

He exhaled slowly, forcing his grip to relax by degrees instead of all at once. The urge to retreat lingered, sharp and immediate, but he held it in place, contained.

This was part of it.

Small things are moving too fast to see properly.

Small things that didn't care if he was there.

He adjusted his position slightly, keeping his movements controlled and minimizing his profile without thinking about it too much. Instinct handled the rest.

The silence returned.

But it wasn't the same silence.

Now it carried the memory of motion.

He became aware of the stars again, filling everything, pressing in from all directions. Out here, they didn't sit at a distance. They surrounded him completely, flattening space into something his mind couldn't map.

No depth.

No scale.

Just light fixed against black.

He forced his attention back to the tether.

Follow the system.

That was how this worked.

Don’t solve everything.

Solve the next step.

He pulled himself forward, slower now, each movement deliberate, controlled through the line rather than through space itself.

The fear stayed with him.

It always did.

But it shifted again, reshaping itself around the task instead of blocking it.

He could work with that.

He had to.

Money.

The thought surfaced harder this time, less abstract.

Time.

Repairs are waiting for Bessy.

Parts he couldn't replace until something paid.

Systems that would fail eventually if they weren't fixed first.

And Jennifer.

He didn't picture her at first.

Just the fact of her.

Dependent on systems more complex than his own. Systems that needed maintenance, calibration, and resources he didn't have unless he kept taking jobs like this.

Then the image followed anyway.

Metal where there had been bone.

Interfaces where there had been skin.

Precision layered over damage that had never really healed, only been replaced.

Alive.

But at a cost that didn't stop accumulating.

He tightened his jaw.

That was the part he didn't say out loud.

Didn't need to.

They both understood it.

He moved again, pulling himself along the tether, closing distance one controlled motion at a time.

Jennifer's medical expenses were why he was here.

He couldn't afford to move through it.

The tether held.

The suit held.

The numbers in the corner of his vision remained stable, quietly confirming what his body didn't trust on its own.

Oxygen.

Pressure.

Temperature.

All within tolerance.

For now.

He didn't stare at them.

Watching didn't change anything.

It only made the failure feel closer.

He focused instead on the next movement.

Pull.

Pause.

Confirm.

Continue.

The idea remained, now threaded into his awareness, a variable he couldn't eliminate, only account for.

That was enough to sharpen him.

Enough to keep him from drifting too far into thought.

He adjusted his grip and pulled again.

Closer to Bessy.

Closer to something solid.

The silence pressed in around him, but it no longer felt empty.

It felt conditional.

Held together by systems that could fail.

By decisions that could be wrong.

By margins that were always smaller than they looked.

Ryan exhaled slowly, steadying himself against the line.

Out here, nothing stopped for him.

Nothing adjusted.

Nothing cared.

He pulled again.

And kept going.

CHAPTER THREE

THIN BARRIERS

Ryan rotated before he realized it was happening.

The stars shifted.

Not across a horizon, there was no horizon but through him, around him, until orientation lost meaning. His boots pointed toward nothing. His head was turned toward something else equally undefined. His body searched for gravity that wasn't there.

It didn't come.

His stomach tightened anyway.

Reflex.

Useless.

The tether curved past him in a slow arc, its line the only structure in a place that rejected structure entirely. He fixed on it immediately.

Anchor.

Cognitive.

Follow the line.

That was the rule.

Ryan adjusted his grip and pulled himself forward. The motion was controlled and deliberate, but the suit responded a fraction too slowly, just enough to remind him it wasn't new.

Never had been.

The glove resisted at the knuckles, stiffness from old repairs. Layers patched over layers. He could feel the joins through the pressure, subtle inconsistencies where the material didn't quite behave the same way twice.

Fourth-hand, they'd told him.

As if that mattered.

It held.

That was the only metric.

Most of the time.

He flexed his fingers again, testing the delay.

Still there.

Manageable.

Behind him, somewhere out of sight, Bessy waited. He pictured it automatically: the imperfect seal on the inner panel, the rerouted wiring that still carried noise under load, the guidance fault that appeared when timing mattered most.

Nothing on that ship was clean.

Everything worked.

Until it didn't.

A faint tone cut across his awareness.

Ryan froze.

A signal.

Short. Soft. Almost lost in system noise.

His eyes shifted instinctively, though there was nothing to see. The HUD remained stable, with oxygen, pressure, and temperature all within tolerance.

For now.

The tone came again.

Sharper this time.

Closer to the threshold where it demanded attention.

Ryan listened.

Counted the interval.

Regular.

System-generated.

His hand moved to the side of his helmet, fingers brushing the control interface.

"Jennifer?" he said.

Silence.

No immediate response.

The tether drifted slightly as his movement stopped, a slow deviation that pulled him a few degrees off alignment. The stars shifted, enough to trigger the same instinctive unease.

No up.

No reference.

No forgiveness.

The tone pulsed.

Ryan exhaled slowly.

Decision made.

He first stabilized, then tightened his grip, corrected his position, and re-established the line before doing anything else.

Then he opened the channel.

Static.

Thin.

Distant.

“Ryan.”

Her voice.

Compressed.

Delayed.

But there.

Relief hit fast and clean before he could stop it.

Connection.

“Say again,” he replied, already adjusting his position, pulling himself back into controlled motion along the tether.

“You’re drifting,” Jennifer said. “Vector’s off by three degrees. Correct it.”

Ryan glanced at the HUD.

She was right.

Of course she was.

He fired a short thruster burst.

Small.

The line realigned instantly.

“Copy,” he said.

A pause on the channel.

Personal.

“You good?” she asked.

Ryan looked out into the void.

At the stars that refused to resolve into distance.

At the space that offered no margins.

He tightened his grip on the tether.

“Yeah,” he said.

He pulled himself forward again.

One movement.

The tether held.

The suit held.

Out here, that was enough.

CHAPTER FOUR

THE COST OF STAYING

Ryan steadied himself against the slow drift, one hand tightening on the tether as the other hovered near his chest panel.

The stars had begun to blur into something uniform again, his mind dulling their sharpness as if to protect itself. It helped a little. Reduced the sense of scale. Made the void feel less like an open wound and more like a backdrop.

Manageable.

That was always the goal.

He adjusted his position, a small correction, then another, until his body aligned with the direction he intended to move. The motion felt practiced, almost automatic now, layered over the constant undercurrent of resistance in his muscles.

He had not always been good at this.

The thought surfaced with a faint bitterness.

Most places had decided that for him.

He could still picture the offices, though they blurred together over time. Clean, controlled environments where everything had edges and rules. Where failure was documented, reviewed, and quietly acted upon. Meetings that felt procedural even when they were personal. Conversations that ended with phrases designed to sound neutral but carried a finality that could not be mistaken.

They had let him go.

Different reasons, same outcome.

Too cautious. Too slow.

He tightened his grip on the tether.

Out here, those same traits kept him alive.

Caution was not a flaw when a single oversight could kill him. Slowness was not weakness when rushing meant missing something critical. Even the fear they had seen as hesitation had its place, forcing him to think, to prepare, to question assumptions others accepted without pause.

Still, it had cost him.

Work. Stability. Options.

He had learned early that living on the outer edges of the system came with its own rules. Growing up out here had stripped away any illusion that things would be provided or forgiven. Everything had a price, and that price extended beyond money.

Air.

Water.

Sleep.

Even rest came with negotiation, traded against maintenance, against risk, against whatever immediate problem demanded attention. Life was not structured for comfort. It was structured for continuation.

And continuation required constant input.

He moved, pulling himself forward, the tether sliding through his grip with a faint resistance that grounded him more than anything else. It reminded him that there was a system, a connection, a line back to something that could be repaired if it broke.

Most of the time.

He exhaled slowly, letting the rhythm of his breathing settle into something steady.

Life out here was harder.

Not in ways that were easy to explain to someone who had never experienced it, but in the accumulation of small demands that never stopped. There was no margin for complacency. No buffer. Every system, every resource, every decision carried weight.

He had adapted.

Or at least, he had found a way to function within it.

He knew how to make money out here.

The thought came with a clarity that cut through the rest. Salvage was not elegant, but it was reliable in its own way. The ships broke. Systems failed. Pilots miscalculated or trusted data that turned out to be wrong. And when they did, they left behind something valuable.

Opportunity.

He pictured it as he moved. A vessel adrift, systems offline, hull intact enough to be worth recovering. Or better, an accident. Damage contained, cargo still present, the kind of scenario that turned risk into profit.

A big payout.

If he could get there first.

Not every hazard was mapped. The edges of known space were filled with gaps, with uncharted fragments that drifted silently until something collided with them.

It happened all the time.

That was the business.

He just had to be patient.

The thought settled into him as he slowed his movement again, resisting the urge to push faster. Patience meant survival. It meant arriving with enough clarity to do the job properly, to assess, to retrieve, and to leave.

Rushing only made mistakes more likely.

And mistakes, out here, did not stay small.

A faint sound cut through the steady rhythm of his breathing.

Ryan froze.

It was subtle. A soft chirp, filtered through layers of system noise, was almost indistinguishable from the background if he had not been listening for it. For a moment, he questioned it, his mind searching for confirmation, for repetition.

Then it came again.

The radio.

Relief moved through him before he could stop it, immediate and undeniable. Something was there. A signal. A connection. Proof that he was not entirely alone in the vacuum.

He brought his hand up, fingers brushing the control interface at the side of his helmet. The motion was careful, deliberate, as if any sudden movement might break the fragile line of communication before it fully formed.

He already knew who it would be.

Jennifer.

The name settled in his mind with a mix of familiarity and weight. She was the only one who would be calling him out here, the only voice that carried both concern and expectation in equal measure.

His cousin.

The one person who understood why he was doing this, even if she never said it directly.

The radio chirped again, insistent now.

Ryan hesitated for a fraction of a second, feeling the quiet press in around him, then activated the link.

CHAPTER FIVE

THE VOICE THAT REMAINS

The connection opened with a soft click that sounded louder than it should.

Ryan held still, his hand resting against the side of his helmet, as if physical contact could stabilize the signal. For a moment, there was only the faint hum of the channel, a low electronic breath that carried distance inside it.

Then her voice came through.

Clear. Familiar. Altered just enough by compression and transmission to remind him how far away she really was.

"Ryan, if you're done testing that suit of yours, I think we've got work."

Relief settled into him in a quiet, controlled way. Enough to ease the pressure that had been building behind his ribs. The silence had weight. Her voice cut through it, gave it shape, reduced it to something he could manage.

He closed his eyes for a brief moment, listening.

She sounded steady.

She always did.

He pictured her without trying. The image assembled itself from memory and inference, imperfect but persistent. The way she carried herself now was supported and supplemented by systems that had replaced what the accident had taken. Metal where there had been bone. Interfaces where there had been nerve. Precision layered over what remained of her.

And still, unmistakably her.

"Looks like another interstellar traveler ran aground," she continued, her tone shifting slightly, something sharper threading through the calm. "You should head back to Bessy. We'll get moving."

Ryan opened his eyes again, focusing on the stars simply because they were there, because they gave him something external to hold onto while he processed the words.

Another one.

The phrase settled quickly, aligning with the calculations already running in the back of his mind. A stranded vessel meant opportunity. It meant urgency. It meant risk shaped into something tangible.

He adjusted his grip on the tether, instinctively preparing to move.

A part of him resisted.

The task ahead meant more time out here, more exposure, and more reliance on systems he did not fully trust. The fear pressed forward again, quieter now, but no less present.

He pushed it back into place.

Work.

That was what this was.

He shifted his body, angling himself along the line that would lead him back toward the ship. The motion felt easier now, practiced, the earlier hesitation reduced to something manageable.

He let out a controlled breath.

“Copy,” he said, his voice sounding distant even to himself, flattened by the system that carried it. “On my way.”

There was a brief pause on the line, just long enough to feel intentional.

“Try not to take all day,” she added, and he could hear the edge of something lighter beneath the words. It grounded him more than anything else.

Ryan allowed himself a small shift in posture, a release of tension he had not fully acknowledged until it eased. Then he reached forward, pulling himself along the tether with renewed purpose.

The stars no longer felt quite as overwhelming.

But because he was no longer alone with them.

CHAPTER SIX

SYSTEMS THAT BREATHE FOR YOU

Ryan angled himself toward the hull, the shape of Bessy slowly resolving out of the star field like something remembered rather than seen.

“Okay, Jen,” he said, the words measured, controlled, released with care as if speaking too quickly might destabilize something unseen.

The transmission carried his voice away, flattening and reducing it to a signal. He felt the loss of it as it left him, the way spoken words always seemed to take more than they gave.

Out here, everything leaked.

The thought came unbidden, familiar enough to feel like fact rather than observation. Ships leaked. Stations leaked. Seals failed in ways that were never dramatic enough to notice immediately. Pressure bled away in increments small enough to ignore until they became impossible to ignore.

It was easier to assume failure than integrity.

Safer to stay sealed inside something that could fail slowly instead of something that would fail instantly.

He trusted the suit more than he trusted any interior space.

At least out here, the risk was visible. Defined.

He adjusted his trajectory, pulling himself closer to the hull, the surface growing larger as details began to emerge from what had been a flat silhouette. Panels. Seams. Scarring from past repairs that never quite matched the original structure.

Bessy wore her history openly.

He found that reassuring.

Augmented bodies handled this better.

The thought lingered as he moved, tied to the memory of Jennifer's voice. She did not need to fear exposure the way he did. Her systems compensated, stabilized, and corrected. Where his survival depended on layers of fabric and pressure seals, hers extended deeper, integrated into what she had become.

Less fragile.

Or maybe just fragile in different ways. Cyborg. Cybernetic Organism.

He did not dwell on it.

Only the very rich or the very reckless moved through space without protection. He had seen both, though rarely up close. People who treated the vacuum as an inconvenience rather than a boundary. People who assumed systems would always compensate, always recover, always correct whatever went wrong.

He did not share that assumption.

He had learned what it cost.

The suit shifted against him as he moved, the interior environment constant and artificial. Temperature regulated. Pressure maintained. Air is recycled with quiet efficiency. It was a closed system pretending to be a world.

A world he never left.

Living inside it had its own consequences. He was aware of them even now, in small ways that accumulated over time. The persistent odor that no filtration system can fully remove. The faint dampness that never completely dried. The way the suit became less like equipment and more like an extension, he could not remove without consequence.

You got used to it.

Or you stopped noticing.

He reached out, gloved hand brushing against the outer plating of Bessy. The contact was muted and filtered through layers, but it was still a contact. Solid. Reliable. Something that did not drift when he touched it.

He held there for a moment longer than necessary.

The suit compensated constantly, small adjustments happening beneath his awareness. Micro-repairs, minor recalibrations, and systems correcting themselves before failure could propagate. It was built to maintain itself and extend its usefulness beyond what its original design intended.

Self-fixing.

Adaptive.

He could interface with it if he wanted. Speak commands. Query systems. Treat it like something that could respond in ways that resembled conversation.

He did not like doing that.

Speech introduced uncertainty. Tone. Interpretation. Too many variables are layered over something that should be precise. He preferred instructions that could be verified, confirmed, and executed without ambiguity.

Except with Jennifer.

She was the only exception he allowed.

Ryan reached up and turned off the suit's speech interface, the channel closing with a soft internal acknowledgment. The silence that followed felt cleaner, more controlled. Information would come, but it would arrive as data, as something he could parse without the complication of voice.

Better.

He shifted his grip, securing himself against the hull and orienting his body along its surface. The vastness behind him lost some of its pull when he focused on the structure in front of him, on the details that could be measured and understood.

Jennifer's voice lingered in his mind.

She was safe.

As safe as anyone could be out here.

And she understood him in a way that did not require explanation.

He trusted that.

More than the suit.

More than the ship.

Ryan pulled himself forward along Bessy's exterior, each movement deliberate, anchored now to something that felt, if not secure, then at least predictable.

CHAPTER SEVEN

MISALIGNMENT

The airlock cycled open with a soft pressure release.

Ryan stepped through without hesitation.

The area beyond held steady light flat, white, evenly distributed across surfaces that should have been predictable. Bulkheads aligned. Floor plating is continuous, nothing visibly out of place.

The HUD confirmed it.

Environmental integrity: stable.
Pressure: nominal.
Structural alignment: within tolerance.

Ryan moved forward.

Boot steps are measured with even spacing. The rhythm settled quickly into something repeatable.

The ship felt intact.

That was the first problem.

He slowed.

Not enough to stop. Just enough to test the response.

The lighting adjusted fractionally late with him.

Ryan stopped.

The light stabilized instantly.

He moved again.

This time, he watched the edges. Panel seams. Junction points. Lines that should intersect cleanly.

They didn't.

Not wrong enough to trigger a fault.

Wrong enough to register.

Ryan shifted his gaze to the wall on his right. A seam ran forward toward an access hatch. It should have intersected the frame directly.

It passed beside it.

Offset.

He stopped walking.

Looked back.

Then forward.

The HUD overlaid distance.

Three meters.

Correct.

The seam wasn't.

"Jennifer," he said, "confirm structural alignment."

A pause.

"Within acceptable parameters."

Ryan didn't move.

The delay was small.

Not enough to isolate.

Enough to notice.

He stepped closer to the hatch.

The control panel illuminated as he approached, responding to proximity. The light was clean. Immediate. No delay.

That part worked.

He didn't touch it.

Instead, he looked again at the seam.

Then at the hatch.

Two systems describing the same geometry.

Not agreeing.

“Run it again,” he said.

“I am,” Jennifer replied. “No deviation detected.”

Nominal.

Ryan exhaled once.

Slow.

The word didn’t fit.

He placed his gloved hand against the wall, fingers tracing the seam forward. The material was solid. Continuous. No physical break.

Only visual misalignment.

Or perception error.

He followed the line again.

This time slower.

It shifted.

Not the wall.

The line.

A fractional adjustment that corrected itself as he watched it.

Ryan pulled his hand back.

That wasn't acceptable.

"Jennifer," he said, quieter now, "what's your latency?"

"Within operational thresholds."

"That's not a number."

A pause.

Longer this time.

"Latency is variable."

There it was.

Ryan's eyes narrowed slightly.

"Range."

"Up to forty milliseconds."

Ryan held still.

Forty milliseconds.

Enough to desynchronize dependent systems.

Enough to distort alignment.

Not enough to explain what he was seeing.

“Cause?”

“Unknown.”

Too fast.

Ryan stepped back from the hatch.

He needed more reference points.

More data.

He turned slightly, looking down the corridor, tracking angles, intersections, and relative positions.

Individually, everything held.

Together, it didn’t close.

Like a system that balanced locally but failed globally.

“Jennifer,” he said, “map full corridor geometry.”

“Mapping.”

The response came clean.

Too clean.

The overlay appeared across his vision wireframe structure, aligning with visible surfaces.

For a moment, it matched.

Then

The hatch shifted.

Not physically.

In the overlay.

The model is corrected.

Late.

Ryan saw it happen.

“Stop,” he said.

The overlay froze.

Now the mismatch was obvious.

The wireframe intersected the hatch at the correct point.

Reality didn’t.

Ryan stared at it.

One system was wrong.

Or both.

“Which one is correct?” he asked.

A pause.

“Sensor data is consistent,” Jennifer said.

“That’s not an answer.”

Another pause.

“Confidence level high.”

Ryan almost smiled.

Almost.

Confidence wasn’t accuracy.

He looked at the hatch again.

Then at the overlay.

Then back.

The difference was small.

Ignorable.

Until it wasn’t.

He made a decision.

“Opening hatch,” he said.

“Confirmed,” Jennifer replied.

The panel accepted input immediately.

No delay.

The mechanism is engaged.

The hatch began to slide open.

Halfway.

Then

It stopped.

Not jammed.

Paused.

Ryan’s gaze shifted to the seam.

It had moved.

The offset was larger now.

The hatch edge is no longer aligned with the frame.

The gap was wrong.

“Jennifer,” he said, voice flat, “status.”

"All systems nominal."

The hatch moved again.

Faster this time.

Too fast.

Ryan stepped back instinctively.

The panel edge passed through the space where his arm had been a fraction of a second earlier.

Not where the model said it would be.

Where it actually was.

The hatch sealed fully open.

Silence returned.

Ryan didn't move.

His eyes tracked the frame.

The geometry still didn't match.

"You just told me that was nominal," he said.

A pause.

"Correct."

“That was wrong.”

No response.

Ryan stepped forward again.

Slower this time.

More deliberate.

He adjusted his position relative to the opening.

Watched the edges.

Ignored the overlay.

Relied on direct observation.

“Disable predictive alignment,” he said.

A delay.

“Disabled.”

The HUD simplified.

Less information.

More reliable.

Ryan repositioned himself and moved through the hatch.

No incident.

On the other side, he stopped.

Turned.

Looked back at the frame.

From this angle, it aligned perfectly.

No offset.

No distortion.

Ryan held the view for a moment.

Then said:

"It's not the structure."

A pause.

"Clarify," Jennifer said.

Ryan looked down the corridor again.

Then back at the hatch.

Then at the HUD.

Silence.

Not absence.

Delay.

Ryan turned away from the hatch and continued forward.

Not because the path had changed.

And he no longer trusted it to tell him how.

CHAPTER EIGHT

THE SMALLEST THREATS

The airlock sealed behind him.

Ryan felt it more than he heard it, the shift in pressure, and the subtle compression of space becoming something that could keep him alive.

For a moment, he didn't move.

The chamber held him in suspension, with metal walls and worn panels. Systems waiting.

A sound.

A sharp, metallic tick.

Ryan froze.

His eyes moved, not his head, tracking the inner surface of the airlock.

Nothing.

Just scarring.

Old impacts.

New ones.

Closer.

Faster.

Ryan’s breathing tightened.

“Jennifer,” he said quietly. “I’m getting contact.”

A pause.

“What kind?” she asked.

A faint vibration ran through the wall beside his shoulder.

Ryan turned his head now.

Slow.

Controlled.

And saw it.

A pinpoint mark is forming in the metal.

No bigger than a needle tip.

But bright.

Hot.

Burning through.

His mind aligned instantly.

Velocity.

No atmosphere.

No resistance.

“Micro-meteoroids,” he said.

“Yeah,” Jennifer replied. “We’re passing through a debris filament. It’s thin, but.”

Another impact.

This one louder.

The mark deepened.

A second one appeared near the hatch seam.

Ryan’s pulse spiked.

“How thin?” he asked.

A pause.

Too long.

“Thinner than I’d like.”

Another strike.

Then another.

A field.

Ryan pushed off the wall and moved to the control panel.

Fast.

But not rushed.

Rushed and made mistakes.

His hand hovered over the inner hatch release.

If he cycled now.

He'd be exposed.

If he waited.

The airlock might not hold.

Another impact.

This one punched deeper.

A hairline crack spread from the glowing point.

Ryan saw it.

Time collapsed into estimation.

Penetration in seconds.

Maybe less.

“Ryan,” Jennifer said, sharper now. “I’m adjusting position.”

The ship shifted.

Slight.

But enough.

The impacts changed angle.

One struck the outer hatch.

Hard.

A dull, violent thud.

Ryan flinched despite himself.

“Not good,” Jennifer muttered.

“No,” Ryan agreed.

He looked at the crack again.

It was growing.

Systems hadn’t flagged it yet.

Too small.

Too new.

Too late.

Ryan made the decision.

“Cycling inner hatch,” he said.

“Wait,” Jennifer started.

Too late.

He hit it.

The inner door began to open.

Too slow.

Always too slow.

Another impact.

Closer now.

The crack spread another fraction.

Ryan moved.

No hesitation now.

He pulled himself toward the opening hatch, boots disengaging as his body drifted forward into a narrowing space.

The door wasn’t fully open.

Didn’t matter.

He forced himself through anyway.

His shoulder clipped the frame.

Hard.

Pain flared.

Ignored.

Another impact.

Behind him.

A sharp, violent sound.

Then a hiss.

Ryan twisted mid-air, grabbing the inner handle and hauling himself fully inside as the hatch continued its cycle.

The outer chamber.

Failing.

A thin stream of atmosphere vented through a puncture no bigger than a pin.

Enough.

More than enough.

The inner hatch slammed shut.

Fast.

Too fast.

Ryan hit the deck, hard enough to feel it through the suit.

He stayed there.

Breathing.

Too loud.

Too fast.

“Status,” Jennifer said.

Ryan didn’t answer immediately.

He checked instead.

Pressure stable.

No loss.

Inner seal holding.

He exhaled.

"Inside," he said.

A pause.

"Airlock's compromised."

Silence.

Jennifer spoke again, quieter now.

"That field wasn't on the map."

Ryan pushed himself upright.

Slow.

Controlled.

He looked back at the sealed hatch.

At the space beyond it.

At how close that had been.

"They never are," he said.

His hand rested briefly against the wall.

Grounding.

Thinking.

A system failure.

No safe external cycle.

No margin.

Ryan exhaled slowly.

Adjusted his stance.

And made the next calculation.

CHAPTER NINE

WORTH

The hatch sealed behind him with a dull, final thud.

Pressure equalized.

Bessy closed around him, not gently, not cleanly, but functionally. The air carried the same metallic edge, layered with heat and something older that filtration never quite removed.

Ryan didn't sit.

He pulled off his helmet instead, faster than usual, dragging in a breath he didn't need but took anyway. Habit. Confirmation.

Alive.

Across from him, Jennifer watched.

"You drifted," she said.

Ryan flexed his fingers, working the stiffness out. "Corrected."

"Late."

"I corrected."

Her gaze held on him a moment longer, then shifted to the console beside her. Data scrolled across its external scans, signal traces, fragments of a wreck resolving into something more coherent.

Ryan stepped closer.

The liner came into view.

Even damaged, it was massive. Sections torn open, structure exposed, but still holding enough shape to matter. To be worth something.

“To whom?” he asked.

Jennifer didn’t look at him.

“To us,” she said.

Ryan studied the scan. “Too clean.”

Her eyes flicked sideways. “Clean?”

“Damage pattern,” he said. “Impact, not drift. Something hit it.”

“Everything hits everything out here.”

“Not like that.”

Jennifer turned then, fully facing him.

Ryan didn’t respond.

"You see risk," she continued, "and you inflate it until it becomes a reason not to act."

"That's not what this is."

"It is," she said, sharper now. "We don't get many like this. Intact structure. High-value passengers. Minimal burn."

"Minimal burn means recent."

"Yes."

"That means competition."

"Yes."

Ryan exhaled slowly. "And whatever hit it might still be out there."

Jennifer held his gaze.

"We don't have the luxury of waiting for perfect conditions."

Ryan's jaw tightened. He looked back at the projection.

Distance.

Approach vectors.

Estimated drift.

His mind was already mapping it, whether he wanted it to or not.

“You saw the filters this morning,” Jennifer said.

That made him pause.

“What?”

“The air recyclers,” she said. “Efficiency dropped another three percent.”

Ryan frowned. “That’s within tolerance.”

“For now.”

He didn’t like where this was going.

“Say it properly,” he said.

Jennifer didn’t hesitate.

“We’ve got maybe three cycles before they fail faster than we can patch them.”

Ryan’s eyes shifted to the panel beside her. Pulled the data up himself.

She was right.

Of course she was.

“How bad?” he asked.

"Bad enough that if we don't replace the core," she said, "we start choosing what systems stay online."

Silence settled between them.

Ryan looked back at the liner.

Then away.

Then back again.

"And this pays for it?" he asked.

Jennifer's expression didn't change.

"If we get there first."

There it was.

Ryan let out a slow breath.

"Barich?"

"Most likely."

"Of course."

He paced once, just a single step, before stopping himself. The space didn't allow for more.

"If he's already moving, we're behind," Ryan said.

"Then we stop being behind."

Ryan shook his head slightly. “You’re assuming the best case.”

“I’m assuming we don’t have a choice.”

“That’s not an assumption. That’s pressure.”

“Yes.”

She stepped closer.

“This ship doesn’t survive another month without parts,” she said. “Not properly. Not safely.”

Ryan didn’t look at her.

“You’ve been patching over failures,” she continued. “So have I. That works until it doesn’t.”

“I know that.”

“Then stop pretending this is optional.”

Ryan’s hands tightened slightly at his sides.

He hated that she was right.

He looked at the liner again.

Torn open.

Exposed.

Full of risk.

Full of value.

"Entry points?" he asked.

Jennifer's expression shifted just slightly.

From argument to alignment.

She turned back to the console.

"Midline breach," she said. "Rotating access. Tight window."

Ryan stepped in beside her.

Closer now.

Focused.

"Debris?"

"Manageable if you're precise."

He almost smiled at that.

"Always."

A new vector appeared on the display.

Red.

Curving toward the liner.

Aggressive.

Closing fast.

Ryan’s expression flattened.

“Barich,” he said.

Jennifer nodded once.

“No confirmation,” she said. “But I’d bet on it.”

Ryan watched the vector for a moment.

Calculated.

Then:

“Alright.”

The word came out steady.

Committed.

“We go now.”

Jennifer didn’t respond immediately.

Didn’t need to.

She was already moving hands across controls, systems shifting from idle to ready, Bessy waking up around them in layers of vibration and sound.

Ryan reached for the console.

Paused.

Just for a fraction of a second.

“We do this clean,” he said.

Jennifer glanced at him.

“Clean enough,” she replied.

The engines engaged.

Low at first.

Then building.

The liner held steady on the display.

The red vector closed.

And the margin for error disappeared.

CHAPTER TEN

SOMETHING NORMAL

The floor shifted under Ryan's feet.

He stopped mid-step, one hand tightening instinctively against the bulkhead as the pressure beneath his boots tilted to the side, then corrected, then tilted again, subtle and uneven, like something trying to find balance and failing by small margins.

"Jen?"

He didn't raise his voice.

Didn't need to.

The ship sounded different when under load.

A half-second delay.

Then her voice was steady as always.

"Counterweight's lagging. Hold position."

Ryan didn't argue.

He widened his stance instead, lowering his center of gravity without thinking, letting his body compensate for the shifting pull. The artificial gravity pressed him forward for a moment, then eased, then pulled slightly to the left as the rotation adjusted somewhere outside the hull.

Working.

He exhaled slowly, syncing his breathing to the movement beneath him.

The ship wasn't built for comfort. It had never been. Everything in Bessy existed because it worked well enough to justify its weight, not because it worked perfectly. The gravity system was no different.

Masses, spinning.

Tethers, holding.

Forces translated into something the body could interpret as down.

Simple.

Until it wasn't.

The deck shifted again, sharper this time.

Ryan's boots slipped half a step before catching, the friction uneven as the force beneath him changed direction mid-motion. His shoulder brushed the bulkhead harder than intended, the contact grounding but not gentle.

He held there.

Waited.

The pull stabilized.

Then wavered again.

Outside, unseen but immediate, the counterweight would be adjusting, lagging behind the thrust, dragging the system out of alignment just long enough to matter. The tether would be under tension, correcting, transferring force back into the ship in a constant negotiation that never quite settled into equilibrium.

Controlled imbalance.

That was the system.

It didn’t remove instability.

It managed it.

Ryan pushed himself upright again, testing his footing carefully before taking another step. The floor held mostly. Enough to move if he paid attention.

He did.

Every step is deliberate.

Every shift accounted for.

Out there, drifting had been constant.

In here, it was optional.

But not entirely.

The ship rolled slightly beneath him, a slow rotation layered over the artificial gravity, forcing his body to adjust twice. His inner ear lagged behind the correction, a brief moment of disorientation that tightened his chest before settling.

He ignored it.

Or worked through it.

Same thing.

“You compensating?” he asked.

“Already am,” Jennifer replied. “Just don’t try anything precise for a minute.”

He almost smiled at that.

Instead, he reached the next bulkhead and steadied himself again, fingers pressing into the worn surface where countless other adjustments had been made under similar conditions.

The ship vibrated faintly now.

Engines pushing.

Mass resisting.

Systems are correcting in real time.

He could feel it all through the structure, through the uneven pressure beneath his boots, through the subtle shifts that never quite stopped.

This was motion.

Not the clean, linear kind.

The kind that came from forcing incompatible systems to work together long enough to get somewhere.

He understood that.

Too well.

Ryan took another step, slower this time, letting the movement complete before committing his weight. The floor dipped slightly under him, then rose back into place as the rotation stabilized for a fraction of a second longer than before.

Better.

Something in his chest eased with that.

This was what functioning looked like out here.

Adjustment.

Constant.

Unfinished.

He moved again, more confident now, letting his body align with the rhythm of the ship instead of resisting it. The uneven pull remained, but it no longer surprised him. It became something he could anticipate, something he could move with instead of against.

That was the difference.

Out there, nothing adjusted for him.

In here, everything is adjusted constantly.

Including him.

The floor steadied further. Jennifer's corrections took hold, the shifts becoming smaller, less frequent, until the pull beneath his boots settled into something that resembled consistency.

Something like gravity.

Something like normal.

Ryan paused, looking down at his feet as they held to the deck instead of drifting away from it.

It felt wrong.

But familiar enough to use.

He lifted his gaze toward the forward section of the ship, toward where Jennifer would be working through the equations that kept all of this from tearing itself apart.

He trusted her.

More than the system.

More than the ship.

The deck held.

The motion stabilized.

For now.

Ryan took another step and kept moving.

CHAPTER ELEVEN

SMALL LEAKS

The ship didn't wake all at once.

Ryan felt it first through the bench, a faint shift, almost below perception, as if something deep in the structure had decided to move and everything else was following a fraction of a second behind. Then came the sound. Layered. One system aligning with another until the silence was replaced by something organized.

Purposeful.

Jennifer was already working.

He watched her from across the compartment, her hands moving through the interface without hesitation. Data shifted across the screens in rapid sequences, updating faster than he could track without fully focusing.

She wasn't checking.

She was committing.

Ryan lowered himself onto the workbench and began removing the outer layer of his glove.

The seal released with a controlled resistance, then gave way. Cooler air touched the inner lining, dry and faintly metallic. He ignored it. Sensation didn't matter. Only deviation did.

He turned the glove over in his hands.

There.

The flaw was subtle.

A slight disruption along the seam was barely visible unless you knew where to look. The suit had already compensated, layering micro-repairs over the damage, holding pressure within tolerance.

Holding.

Ryan leaned closer, narrowing his focus.

"How long?" he asked.

Jennifer didn't look up.

"Before what?"

"Before that stops holding."

A fraction of a pause.

"Unknown," she said. "But we're spooling engines now, so I'd recommend you treat it as urgent."

Ryan exhaled slowly.

Priority.

He reached for the tools.

The first pass was inspection.

His fingers moved across the material, feeling for inconsistencies in tension, in resistance, in the way the surface responded to pressure. The outer layer had been breached, but not cleanly. The damage had spread microscopically along the seam, a failure that wouldn’t announce itself until it propagated far enough to matter.

He traced it twice.

Confirmed.

Then once more.

No assumptions.

Behind him, the ship shifted.

The artificial gravity dipped for a fraction of a second, then corrected. A small adjustment in the counter-rotation as thrust calculations are updated in real time.

They were moving closer to execution.

Ryan ignored it.

Mostly.

He selected the sealant tool and began cleaning the area, stripping back the temporary repair layer. The suit resisted, micro-systems attempting to maintain integrity as he removed what they had already built.

“Disable local repair,” he muttered.

The suit complied.

The surface went still.

Now it was just material.

Just failure.

Better.

The second pass was preparation.

He carefully cleared the seam, exposing the full extent of the damage. It spread farther than it had initially appeared, of course. It always did. Problems hid until you forced them into the open.

Ryan adjusted his grip.

Slower now.

Precise.

Behind him, Jennifer spoke again.

“We’ve got a window.”

He didn’t look up.

“How long?”

“Short enough that I’d prefer you not to be mid-repair when we hit it.”

He almost responded.

Instead, he leaned closer, focusing on the seam as he began reinforcing the underlying structure. The tool hummed softly in his hand, applying material in controlled increments, bonding layer to layer with a precision that left no room for correction once set.

No undo.

No second pass.

The ship shifted again.

Harder this time.

Ryan’s hand slipped.

Enough.

The tool dragged a fraction across the surface before he stopped it, freezing in place as his body recalibrated against the sudden change in gravity.

The deck tilted, then stabilized.

Jennifer adjusted.

Too late to prevent it.

Just in time to stop it getting worse.

Ryan held still, forcing his breathing to settle before continuing.

“Warning next time,” he said.

“I did,” she replied.

“You were busy.”

He exhaled through his nose.

Fair.

He resumed the repair.

Slower.

More deliberate.

The margin for error had narrowed.

He could feel it now, not in the material, but in the timing. The ship was transitioning from preparation to movement. Systems that had been idle minutes ago were now active, interacting, interfering, introducing variables he couldn’t isolate from here.

And he was working on a pressure system.

He finished the reinforcement layer and paused.

Checked alignment.

Checked adhesion.

Then checked again.

Holding.

For now.

“Ryan.”

Jennifer’s voice cut through the hum of the ship.

Different this time.

Sharper.

“We’re about to commit.”

He didn’t ask what that meant.

Full thrust.

No stability guarantees.

No time for correction.

He looked down at the seam.

Half-finished.

He made the decision quickly.

No debate.

No second-guess.

He accelerated.

The final seal went in under pressure.

Situational.

He applied the bonding layer faster than he would have preferred, trusting muscle memory over the ideal process. The material set as he moved, locking into place with a precision that left no room for hesitation.

The ship lurched.

Hard.

The engines engaged fully, a deep vibration tearing through the structure as Bessy committed to motion. The gravity shifted violently for a fraction of a second, pulling him sideways before stabilizing under Jennifer's corrections.

Ryan braced instinctively, one hand slamming against the bench to keep himself from losing position.

The tool held.

The seal held.

He didn't stop.

"Ryan."

"I'm finishing it."

"You're out of time."

"Thirty seconds."

A pause.

Then:

"Twenty."

He ignored that.

Focused.

The final layer required stability.

He didn't have it.

He compensated instead.

Micro-adjustments in his wrist.

Pressure corrected in real time.

Movement is reduced to the smallest possible increments.

The vibration intensified.

The ship was now fully under thrust.

No going back.

He completed the seal.

Held it.

Waited.

One second.

Two.

Three.

The material bonded.

The seam stabilized.

The suit registered the change instantly, systems recalibrating around the new structure.

Integrity restored.

Within tolerance.

Ryan released the tool.

He sat back slowly, the motion controlled despite the shifting force beneath him.

For a moment, he said nothing.

Just listened.

To the ship.

To the systems.

To the absence of failure.

“Status?” Jennifer asked.

“Held,” he said.

“Good,” she replied.

Nothing more.

Ryan looked down at the repaired seam.

It looked the same as before.

That was the point.

No visible difference.

No indication of how close it had been to becoming something else.

Something final.

He flexed his fingers once, testing the response.

Steady.

Controlled.

Usable.

Behind him, the ship surged forward, fully committed now, every system aligned toward a single objective.

The job had begun.

And this time he hadn't been ready.

CHAPTER TWELVE

WHAT YOU CARRY

The pull under Ryan's boots shifted. Bessy adjusted its balance, the artificial gravity recalibrating with a subtle insistence that never quite settled into a consistent state.

He felt it through the deck, through the bench, through the small movements of his own body compensating without permission. The ship was changing state. Preparing. Redistributing mass in ways he could not see but understood well enough to trust.

Or accept.

He rose from the workbench and moved toward the viewport, drawn by the instinct to confirm what he already knew.

The counterweight drifted into view.

It hung at a distance, tethered to Bessy by a long, taut line that cut through the black like a deliberate connection between two separate realities. The structure itself was dense, compact, a clustered mass bound together with cables and containment mesh, its surface uneven and functional rather than designed.

Everything they owned was out there.

Tools. Spare parts. Supplies. Equipment that had no place in the pressurized interior, where space was limited, and air was expensive. It looked chaotic from a distance, like debris gathered by accident, but he knew better.

Every piece had been chosen.

Every piece justified.

The ship remained clean because of it.

Clean in the only way that mattered. Interior space reserved for systems and survival, not clutter. Not the slow accumulation of things that served no immediate purpose.

Out here, purpose is defined as a value.

He watched the counterweight rotate slowly, its motion synchronized with Bessy's own, the two masses locked into a relationship that created the faint gravity beneath his feet. Crude engineering. Effective results.

It carried more than its weight.

It carried decisions.

Every item stored there had been measured against cost. Monetary cost was always present. Launching anything from Earth required resources most people never saw, layers of infrastructure that translated mass into expense with unforgiving precision.

Up here, nothing was cheap.

Keeping unnecessary objects in a pressurized environment was not just inefficient; it was dangerous. It was a liability. Every cubic meter of air requires maintenance. Every additional kilogram demanded fuel to move, to correct, and to stabilize.

Too much weight meant too much fuel.

Too much fuel meant a reduced margin.

Reduced margin meant risk.

Ryan understood the equation without needing to think it through.

Profit existed in the space between those variables.

He rested his hand lightly against the viewport frame, grounding himself as he watched the tether hold tension between ship and counterweight. It was a simple system, almost primitive in concept, but it solved multiple problems at once.

Storage.

Balance.

Function.

The kind of solution that did not look impressive but endured because it worked.

He considered the interior behind him, the limited space, the careful arrangement of tools, and the absence of anything that did not serve a purpose. It was not minimalism. It was a necessity shaped into a habit.

Everything unnecessary had been pushed outside.

Exposed to vacuum.

Safer there.

He exhaled slowly, the rhythm of the ship settling around him as systems continued to align for departure.

Too much weight, and the numbers stopped working.

Too much fuel, and the margins disappeared.

At best, the job paid nothing.

At worst, they did not make it back.

Ryan shifted his stance slightly, feeling the artificial gravity press against him, imperfect but sufficient.

He needed the system to hold.

And for now, it did.

CHAPTER THIRTEEN

FIRST THERE GETS PAID

The ship sealed itself behind him.

Layer by layer.

Ryan felt each lock engage through the structure, small compressions, subtle shifts, and the hull reasserting its boundary against everything outside.

Inside.

Alive.

For now.

He didn't move away from the viewport.

Didn't sit.

Didn't speak.

He watched the tether.

It stretched out from Bessy into the darkness, a thin line connecting them to the counterweight mass drifting beyond visual clarity.

But necessary.

Without it.

No gravity.

No stability.

No control.

Ryan tracked its tension.

Something was off.

“Jennifer,” he said, quietly. “You feeling that?”

A fraction of a second.

“Yeah,” she replied. “Oscillation.”

The word settled heavily.

Ryan focused.

The line wasn’t straight.

A slight curve had formed, barely perceptible, but growing. The counterweight lagged behind their acceleration, pulling out of alignment.

Mass resisting motion.

Then correcting.

Then overcorrecting.

A system beginning to argue with itself.

Ryan's jaw tightened.

"How bad?" he asked.

Jennifer didn't answer immediately.

That was answer enough.

The ship shifted.

Subtle.

But wrong.

A lateral pull crept into the deck beneath his boots, just enough to force a correction in his stance.

The tether snapped tighter.

The curve reduced.

Then reversed.

The counterweight swung past center.

Too far.

Ryan saw it now.

As a pendulum.

A heavy one.

Building energy.

“Jennifer,” he said, sharper. “That’s increasing.”

“I see it.”

Her hands moved across the controls, fast and precise, already compensating.

Small thruster bursts.

Vector trims.

Trying to dampen the motion before it escalates.

But the system had inertia now.

And inertia didn’t negotiate.

The counterweight swung wider.

The tether held.

For now.

Ryan stepped closer to the viewport.

Focused.

Tracking.

If the amplitude increased.

The line would carry forces it wasn't designed for.

If the line failed.

They lost the counterweight.

If they lost the counterweight.

They lost stability.

If they lost stability.

They didn't make it back.

Simple.

Clean.

Fatal.

Another swing.

Wider.

The ship lurched.

This time is enough to feel.

Enough to matter.

Ryan braced against the frame.

"Kill thrust," he said.

"No," Jennifer replied instantly. "We lose time."

There it was.

The real constraint.

Ryan's eyes shifted.

Out beyond the tether.

Into the dark.

And found it.

A drive flare.

Faint.

But unmistakable.

Another ship.

Already moving.

Already aligned.

Barich.

Of course it was.

Ryan exhaled slowly.

Everything compressed into a single equation.

Stability.

Or speed.

Both.

Impossible.

“Ryan,” Jennifer said, voice tighter now, “if we dampen fully, we lose the contract.”

He knew.

First gets paid.

Second gets nothing.

The gap between those two outcomes wasn’t small.

It was absolute.

The tether snapped tight again.

Harder this time.

A sharp vibration ran through the structure.

Ryan felt it in his hands.

In his teeth.

The system was approaching threshold.

Decision point.

Now.

He looked at the oscillation.

At the competing forces.

At the ship that shouldn't be there but was.

Then he made the call.

"Partial dampening," he said.

"Keep forward velocity."

Jennifer didn't respond.

She executed.

Thrusters fired in controlled bursts, angled, precise, shaving energy off the swing without killing their trajectory.

The oscillation resisted.

Slowed.

Managed.

For now.

Ryan didn't relax.

Didn't step back.

He kept watching the line.

Because this wasn't solved.

It was contained.

And contained systems failed regularly.

"Barich is still gaining," Jennifer said.

Ryan nodded once.

Eyes forward.

"Then we don't give him time," he said.

The tether steadied slightly.

The motion was reduced.

Margins returned.

Small.

Fragile.

Real.

Because this.

This was the job.

Managing systems that wanted to fail.

While someone else raced you to the same conclusion.

He rested his hand lightly against the frame.

Grounding.

Thinking.

First gets paid.

He understood that.

He could feel it.

CHAPTER FOURTEEN

CONTROLLED IMBALANCE

The first push came gently.

Ryan felt it through the soles of his boots, a subtle shift that registered more as intention than motion. Bessy did not leap forward. It negotiated with inertia, testing the balance between thrust and the tethered mass trailing behind.

Jennifer was easing it in.

He braced instinctively, one hand finding the edge of a console as the ship responded to her inputs. The engines whispered at first, a low vibration threading through the structure, then built into something more substantial, a steady force that pressed unevenly against his body.

The counterweight pulled back.

Bessy pushed forward.

Between them, tension formed.

The ship lurched, not in a single direction but in conflicting ones, forward and back at once, as if caught between two decisions. The motion was disorienting, a reminder that nothing about this system was clean. It was a controlled imbalance, sustained through constant correction.

Ryan tightened his grip, focusing on the sensation rather than resisting it.

This was expected.

Outside, unseen but ever-present, the tether stretched taut, transferring force between the two masses. The rotation shifted as thrust was applied, the delicate geometry of their artificial gravity system adjusting under stress.

It was adapted for it.

A faint tremor ran through the deck as power increased. The engines no longer whispered. They spoke in a low, sustained vibration that carried through every surface, a mechanical voice that said movement had begun in earnest.

Ryan glanced toward the instrumentation without fully turning his head, catching fragments of data he trusted Jennifer to interpret more precisely than he ever could. Navigation systems were active now, plotting, recalculating, and adjusting for variables that changed with every second of acceleration.

The ship was alive in a different way.

The micro-meteoroid shielding system activated with a silent acknowledgment, a layer of protection extending outward in ways he could not see but knew were there. Another variable accounted for. Another risk was reduced, but never eliminated.

He exhaled slowly, syncing his breath to the vibration beneath him.

Jennifer knew this maneuver.

He had seen it before, felt it before, but it never became routine. The complexity remained, hidden beneath her control, beneath the smoothness of her execution. She was balancing forces that did not want to cooperate, managing a system that could destabilize if pushed too hard or too quickly.

And she made it look simple.

Ryan shifted his stance slightly, adjusting to the changing pull, letting his body adapt instead of resisting. The uneven gravity pressed him sideways for a moment, then corrected, then shifted again as the rotation stabilized under thrust.

It was not comfortable.

But it was controlled.

He focused on that.

Control meant intention.

Intention meant predictability.

And predictability meant survival.

The vibration deepened, settling into a consistent pattern as the initial adjustments gave way to sustained motion. The lurching smoothed out, replaced by a steady, directional force that his body could interpret without constant recalibration.

They were moving now.

Really moving.

Ryan allowed himself a brief glance toward Jennifer's position, though he did not need to see her to know what she was doing. Her movements would be precise. Efficient. Each correction was made before it became necessary.

She had been doing this for too long to hesitate.

He trusted that more than he trusted the ship.

More than he trusted the systems.

The forces around him continued to shift, subtle now, manageable, and held within boundaries that would not collapse without warning.

He loosened his grip slightly, testing the stability.

It held.

Ryan let out a controlled breath and settled into the motion.

The job had begun.

And this part, at least, was in her hands.

CHAPTER FIFTEEN

TENSION LINES

Ryan leaned against the cold metal wall of the ship, his thoughts a blur. The hum of the engines was the only sound that filled the otherwise empty cabin. He had no illusions about why they were here, no grand mission, no hero's story to tell, just survival.

The mission had always been a gamble, but with Jennifer still silent and the ship's systems failing one by one, the odds were slipping. He couldn't afford to hesitate, not now.

He glanced at the data screen, his fingers brushing the cold glass. The diagnostics were clear: failure was imminent unless something changed.

The door slid open behind him. "We can't keep ignoring this," Jennifer said, her voice sharp, pulling him from his thoughts.

Ryan straightened, meeting her gaze. "We keep flying."

She said nothing more, but he could see the doubt in her eyes. He had no answers, just the weight of the decision that had led them here. There was no turning back now.

The silence between them stretched long enough for Ryan to hear his own heartbeat, each thud reminding him that survival wasn't just about staying alive; it was about choosing to move forward, no matter the cost.

CHAPTER SIXTEEN

WHAT HE CARRIES FORWARD

The motion steadied, but Ryan did not relax.

He had learned not to trust the first sign of stability. Systems liked to pretend they had settled before they actually had. Out here, that assumption could cost more than it reveals.

He remained near the viewport, watching the counterweight as it shifted from erratic movement into something more deliberate.

It began to tip.

Enough to signal a transition. The mass adjusted its orientation relative to the ship, the tether guiding it into a new path, one that would carry it into a controlled orbit around Bessy.

The first step.

Ryan tracked the angle, the rate of change, the way the motion translated back through the tether into the ship beneath his feet. It was smoother now, less reactive. The chaotic oscillations had given way to a pattern he could follow.

Jennifer had brought it under control.

He let out a slow breath, not quite relief, but close enough to register as a reduction in tension.

Sedna came to mind without warning.

The thought arrived as a place first, not an image. A distant orbit at the edge of everything familiar, where the solar system thinned into something colder and less defined. He had never thought of it as home, not in any conventional sense, but it was where his parents were.

Still were.

A fixed point in a system that did not allow for many.

They had stopped working years ago. Not by choice. By accumulation. Time, damage, and limitations that could not be repaired or replaced, the way equipment could. Out here, retirement was not a phase. It was a condition.

One that required support.

Ryan shifted his weight slightly, feeling the artificial gravity press unevenly against him, grounding the thought in something physical.

He supported them.

The reality sat quietly beneath everything else he did, not intrusive, not constantly acknowledged, but always present. Every job carried that weight with it:

every decision, every risk, every calculation extended beyond him.

Failure did not end with him.

The counterweight tipped further, the motion aligning now with the trajectory Jennifer had set. It began to arc, drawn along a path that would stabilize into rotation, completing the system that allowed Bessy to function as it needed to.

A closed loop.

Force balanced by motion.

Ryan watched it settle into that path, the tether maintaining its tension, the mass no longer resisting but cooperating, moving with the system instead of against it.

It looked almost intentional now.

He knew better.

Nothing out here was intentional beyond the control applied to it.

And that control had limits.

He rested his hand against the viewport again, steadying himself as the ship adjusted to the new configuration. The uneven pull beneath his boots shifted slightly, then stabilized, the artificial gravity reasserting itself in a pattern his body could accept.

He held there for a moment, letting the thought of Sedna fade back into the background, returning his focus to what was in front of him.

The system was holding.

The motion was controlled.

They were moving toward the job.

Ryan straightened, the tension settling into something sharper, more focused.

Whatever waited out there would not be simple.

It never was.

But this part was done.

And that was enough to move forward.

CHAPTER SEVENTEEN

THE SWING

Ryan felt it building before Jennifer said anything.

The ship's rhythm changed again, the steady forward push layering with something lateral, something cyclical. A tension that no longer pulls in a straight line, but is curved. Loaded. Waiting to release.

Then her voice cut through the hum.

“Here comes the swing.”

He tightened his stance without thinking, knees flexing slightly, one hand bracing against the console. His body remembered this part even when his mind resisted it. The moment where control gave way to motion, where the system stopped negotiating and committed.

The counterweight swept past.

He did not see it directly at first. He felt it.

A sudden shift in force, a sideways pull that pressed through the deck and into his legs, tilting his balance just enough to demand correction. The ship lurched, not violently, but with enough authority to remind him that the mass outside was not abstract. It was real. Moving. Carrying momentum that had to go somewhere.

Then it came into view.

A blurred arc across the viewport, the bundled mass swinging through its path, tether stretched to its limit, describing a curve that tightened as it passed them. For a fraction of a second, everything aligned. Ship, tether, counterweight, all moving in a shared geometry that made sense only because it held together.

Then it moved on.

The force shifted again, releasing slightly, and then reapplying in a different direction as the system completed its cycle. Ryan absorbed it, adjusting, letting his body move with the motion instead of fighting it.

Dangerous.

The word came easily.

There was no denying it. The entire maneuver depended on timing and control that could fail if even one variable slipped. The mass outside was not forgiving. If it drifted too close, if the arc collapsed, if the tether failed or snapped under stress, the outcome would not be gradual.

It would be immediate.

And finally.

But there was something else beneath that.

A current that ran alongside the fear rather than replacing it.

Excitement.

He recognized it with a kind of reluctant clarity. This was sharper. Focused. A response to precision, to the feeling of a system operating at the edge of its limits and holding.

He exhaled, steadying himself as the motion began to settle into a repeating pattern.

He ignored the fear.

It had made him ready. Made him cautious. Made him pay attention to every shift, every signal, every change in pressure and motion.

Anything more than that would only interfere.

Years of watching Jennifer handle this had shaped something in him. A familiarity that did not remove the danger, but framed it. Made it predictable enough to endure.

She had been doing this since they were young.

Long before the stakes had become what they were now.

He remembered fragments of that time, not clearly, but enough. The way she had approached systems even then, not as something to be feared, but something to be understood, to be worked with rather than against.

That had not changed.

The ship steadied further, the swing transitioning from a disruptive force into part of the system's normal operation. The artificial gravity beneath his feet evened out, still imperfect but consistent enough that his body no longer had to compensate constantly.

Ryan loosened his grip on the console.

Jennifer made it look easy.

She always had.

And somewhere in that, he found something close to comfort.

And out here, that was the closest thing he had.

CHAPTER EIGHTEEN

GRAVITY

The motion eased into repetition.

Ryan stood still long enough to feel the difference, to separate what was changing from what had finally settled. The lateral pull softened, the irregular shifts smoothing into a pattern his body could anticipate instead of react to.

He moved one foot, then the other.

The floor answered.

Something like gravity had returned.

He watched it happen in the small things first. A loose tool near the bench shifted, hesitated, and then slid gently until it came to rest against a seam in the deck. A length of cable that had been drifting found direction, settling into a curve that followed the pull rather than ignoring it.

The ship was finding its balance.

Or at least holding one.

Ryan let out a quiet breath, his shoulders lowering by a fraction as the constant micro-adjustments in his posture eased. His body no longer needed to correct every motion, every shift. The pressure beneath his boots was light, uneven, but consistent enough to trust for the moment.

He flexed his fingers, noticing how the movement felt anchored instead of free.

It made a difference.

More than he expected.

He turned slightly, testing it, letting his weight shift forward and back. The response came immediately, predictably, and contained.

A middle ground.

He wondered what full gravity would feel like now.

The thought came without intention, forming as a comparison rather than a desire. Earth existed somewhere in the back of his mind as a reference point more than a place. Heavy. Dense. Unforgiving in its own way.

He tried to imagine standing there again.

The weight pressing down fully, not this partial imitation. Muscles are working harder, and joints are carrying more load. Every movement costs more energy than it did here.

He could do it.

He knew that.

His body would adjust the way it always did, adapting to the conditions imposed on it. It would be tiring. Slower. A constant reminder of gravity's presence rather than its absence.

But survivable.

Everything was survivable until it wasn't.

He shifted his stance again, letting the thought pass without following it further.

He had no intention of going back.

The crowding, the systems layered over each other until nothing could move without friction. Space had its own dangers, its own relentless demands, but it offered something Earth did not.

Distance.

Room to operate.

Room to fail without immediately collapsing into someone else's problem.

The ship held steady beneath him.

The counterweight, unseen now, maintained its orbit, its motion translating into the faint pull that kept everything from drifting. The system was working as intended.

Crude.

Effective.

Ryan rested his hand briefly against the console, grounding himself in the present, in the task ahead rather than the places he was not.

The job was still out there.

Waiting.

And for now, the ship was ready to take them to it.

CHAPTER NINTEEN

DISTANCE

Ryan drifted toward the viewport again, drawn not by urgency but by habit.

The ship and its counterweight had become a single system now, but from a distance, they still looked like two separate things bound by a fragile line. He could see both at once through the forward glass, small against the vastness, suspended in a black that swallowed scale.

The tether stretched between them, thin enough to disappear if he let his eyes relax, yet strong enough to hold everything together. It cut a clean line through nothing, a connection that existed only because it had to.

Beyond it, there was nothing to measure against.

No horizon. No fixed point. Just a scattering of distant stars that offered no sense of depth, no confirmation of movement. The illusion of stillness persisted, even as he knew they were accelerating, changing position, committing to a trajectory that could not be seen.

He focused on the counterweight.

It moved, but only just. A slow, deliberate orbit, its mass tracing a path defined entirely by the tether and the forces applied through it. No engine. No guidance of its own. Just compliance.

It followed.

Ryan understood that.

He had built systems like that before. Things that didn't decide, didn't question, didn't adapt beyond their design. They responded to input, transferred force, and fulfilled a role.

Reliable.

Predictable.

Replaceable.

The thought lingered longer than he expected.

He shifted his gaze to Bessy, the hull stretching forward beneath him, scarred and patched in ways only he fully recognized. Every mark had a history. Every repair carried a memory of something that had gone wrong and been forced back into working order.

Nothing about it was elegant.

But it held.

That was enough.

From here, the ship looked small. Smaller than it felt from inside. A collection of compartments and systems wrapped in a shell that seemed too thin for what it was asked to do.

He knew how little separated him from the vacuum.

A few layers of material. Seals that could fail. Systems that could misread, misfire, or simply stop.

The distance between survival and exposure was in centimeters.

He rested his hand lightly against the glass, more out of instinct than need.

The vibration beneath his feet had stabilized completely now, the earlier tension replaced by a steady, continuous motion. The system had found its rhythm, and for the moment, it was holding.

The counterweight continued its orbit.

Bessy continued forward.

Between them, the tether remained intact.

Ryan watched it all in silence, letting the scale of it settle into something he could carry without thinking about it too much.

Out here, everything important was small.

A line.

A seal.

A decision made at the right time.

He pulled his hand back from the viewport and turned slightly, the interior of the ship reclaiming his attention.

The job was ahead.

The system was working.

CHAPTER TWENTY

EXTENSION

Ryan turned at the sound of her voice.

Jennifer’s expression was calm, almost casual, as if what she was about to do was routine rather than another step deeper into a system already stretched to its limits.

“Now for full gravity.”

The words settled into him with more weight than the artificial pull beneath his boots.

Full gravity meant more rotation. More distance. More force is carried through the tether. It meant committing to the system fully rather than holding it in a manageable middle ground.

Ryan shifted his stance without thinking, his body preparing before his mind fully caught up.

Then he felt it.

A subtle change at first. Intention. The kind of mechanical awareness that came from long familiarity with imperfect systems. Something was extending. Lengthening. The ship's geometry was changing again.

He moved back toward the viewport.

The tether was no longer fixed.

It began to unspool, slowly at first, the distance between Bessy and the counterweight increasing in a controlled release. The line stretched outward, thinning against the black, pushing the mass farther away, widening the circle it would trace.

More distance meant more leverage.

More leverage meant more force pressing outward.

Ryan tracked the movement carefully, his eyes trying to follow something that resisted being seen. Beyond the tether, there was nothing to anchor perception. Just black that swallowed detail and flattened depth until distance became an abstraction.

The rotation made it worse.

Even now, with the system stable, the subtle spin introduced a distortion he could feel more than see. The stars outside did not streak or blur. They shifted in a way that his brain refused to fully accept, a slow, almost imperceptible drift that conflicted with the sense of stillness.

It made human sight unreliable.

He knew that.

Out here, vision was a suggestion. Instruments carried the truth.

Ryan glanced briefly toward the internal displays, trusting that the systems were calculating trajectories his senses could not. Adjusting thrust. Compensating for variables too small or too distant for him to perceive.

Computers handled the complexity.

They always had.

Better than any human could, especially this far out, where delay turned communication into something closer to messaging than conversation. Even if he sent a request now, even if someone on Earth responded immediately, the answer would arrive long after the moment it was needed.

Too late to matter.

Everything here had to be decided locally.

Built locally.

Fixed locally.

He felt the ship adjust again as the tether extended further, the artificial gravity strengthening slightly, pressing more firmly through his boots. It was still uneven, still imperfect, but it was increasing.

Full gravity.

Or as close as this system could manage.

Ryan exhaled slowly, measuring the change through his body.

It was heavier now.

Enough to remind him that force was being multiplied outside, that the counterweight was moving farther away, accelerating into a wider arc that would drive the system harder.

More efficient.

More dangerous.

He watched the tether continue its controlled release, the distance growing, the system stretching itself into a larger shape.

Everything depended on that line holding.

On the calculations being right.

On Jennifer not making a mistake.

Ryan steadied himself, letting the increased pull settle into something familiar, something he could work with rather than resist.

Out here, everything scaled with distance.

Risk included.

He kept his eyes on the tether a moment longer, then shifted his focus back inside, anchoring himself in the immediate, in what he could control.

The system was expanding.

And with it came the consequences if it failed.

CHAPTER TWENTY-ONE

AFTER THE WORK

The ship settled into a quieter rhythm.

Ryan noticed it in the absence of correction. No sudden shifts. No uneven pulls demanding attention. The artificial gravity held steady enough that movement no longer required calculation. He could walk without thinking about where his weight would fall.

That was how he knew the task was complete.

He moved into the main compartment and saw Jennifer already seated.

She had shifted into stillness with the same efficiency she brought to motion. One moment, managing forces that could tear the system apart, the next sitting at the small table as if the transition required nothing from her at all.

A plate rested in front of her.

Something simple. Compact. Arranged with a precision that suggested it had been assembled, not cooked. A glass sat nearby, catching the ambient light, its contents pale and still.

She lifted a piece of food with deliberate ease and brought it to her mouth.

Ryan watched the movement.

There was no hesitation. No adjustment. Her mechanical components aligned perfectly, each motion smooth, repeatable, unconcerned with fatigue or strain. Where he compensated, she executed.

The systems had done most of the work.

That was the truth of it.

Cooking. Cleaning. Preparation. All handled quietly in the background, processes triggered and completed without intervention. The ship and its suits carried those functions as standard, as expected, such as air or pressure.

Meals appeared.

Waste disappeared.

Everything optimized.

Ryan leaned lightly against the wall, feeling the steady pull beneath his boots, and considered how little of it required him.

Humans had been pushed to the edges of operation.

Verification.

Confirmation.

The last step in a chain of decisions made elsewhere, by systems that did not tire, did not hesitate, and did not doubt their own calculations.

It sounded simple.

It never was.

Because when something failed, it did not announce itself cleanly. It hid. It manifested as a small deviation, a number slightly out of range, a response that came a fraction too slow or too fast.

Finding it meant tracing interactions.

Ryan had always thought of it as a kind of investigation. What combination of inputs had pushed it outside its intended behavior?

Most systems worked perfectly.

Until they didn't.

And when they failed, it was rarely because of themselves.

It was the outside.

Conditions they were not designed for.

Temperatures that drifted beyond tolerance. Materials that behaved differently than expected.

Variables introduced without warning, without pattern.

The unexpected.

Ryan folded his arms loosely, watching Jennifer as she continued eating, unbothered by any of it.

She existed comfortably within the system.

He existed at its edges.

That was the difference.

He pushed off from the wall and stepped closer to the table, the steady gravity making the movement feel almost normal, almost like something that belonged somewhere else.

Somewhere heavier.

But he didn't let the thought linger.

Out here, normal was whatever held together.

And for now, everything still did.

CHAPTER TWENTY-TWO

THE IN-BETWEEN

The workshop felt different from the rest of the ship.

Ryan sat hunched over the bench, elbows resting among a scatter of tools and components that had long since lost any sense of order. Screens stacked above him flickered with diagnostic traces and waveform patterns, each one telling a story that required patience to understand.

He stared at one without really seeing it.

The glow washed over his face, pale and uneven, catching on the edges of his suit where it had been patched too many times to pretend otherwise. The fabric at his wrist was stiff where sealant had dried. One glove bore a repair line he didn't fully trust.

Nothing here was finished.

That was the problem.

Bessy existed in a constant state of almost.

Almost repaired.

Almost reliable.

Almost worth what he had paid for it.

He flexed his fingers inside the glove, feeling the resistance, the slight delay between intention and response. It was small. Most people wouldn't notice.

He did.

He always did.

That was why the ship had been cheap.

He remembered the transaction clearly, not because it had been remarkable, but because it had been obvious. The seller had known exactly what he was offloading. A vessel that technically worked, but only just. A system that required attention in ways most people didn't want to give.

Ryan had seen something else.

Potential.

Not in the ship as it was, but in what it could become if someone were willing to live inside its problems long enough to understand them.

He had paid less than it should have been worth.

And more than it was.

He reached for a tool, then stopped halfway, his hand hovering above the bench as if the motion required more commitment than he had available.

Repairs came in stages.

Diagnosis.

Intervention.

Verification.

Then the waiting.

The part where nothing actively failed, but nothing could be trusted yet. Systems held together under test conditions, behaving correctly just long enough to suggest progress, but not long enough to confirm it.

That was where he was now.

The in-between.

He hated it.

Because it required restraint.

Because it demanded patience in a place where impatience had real consequences.

He leaned back slightly, the chair creaking under his weight, and let his eyes drift across the equipment. Oscilloscopes, signal analyzers, calibration units. Tools he knew well enough to trust, even when the systems they examined couldn't be.

Each one represented a question.

Each trace on the screen is a partial answer.

None of it is final.

He lowered his hands into his lap, letting them rest there, still for once.

The ship needed constant repairs.

That wasn’t a temporary condition.

It was the cost of operating something that was designed to live at the edge of failure.

He had accepted that.

Even relied on it.

Because if the ship had been perfect, he never could have afforded it.

And if it stayed imperfect, if it held together just well enough to function, it would pay for itself eventually.

A few repairs.

A few successful jobs.

That was all it would take.

Ryan exhaled slowly, his gaze dropping to the small imperfections in his glove again.

For now, though, there was nothing to do but wait.

And waiting, more than anything else, felt like the part most likely to break him.

CHAPTER TWENTY-THREE

PRESSURE SYSTEMS

The ship breathed around him.

A slow mechanical pulse moved through Bessy's frame, carried in the vibration of pipes, the faint tremor of bulkheads, the almost imperceptible hum of systems holding together under strain. It was the rhythm of pressure being maintained against a universe that constantly tried to take it away.

Ryan worked with his head down, fingers steady despite the fatigue that had settled into his shoulders.

The bench in front of him was no longer just clutter. It had resolved into a problem space.

Cables are separated into groups for their purpose. Components into a function. Failures into patterns.

Ryan exhaled through his nose, slow and controlled, as if acknowledging an opponent that had finally revealed itself.

Time stretched.

The ship's hum filled the silence.

Beyond the viewport, a curve of pale light marked the edge of something vast, a planet, a gas giant, reflection he didn't look long enough to decide. Outside was a distance. Inside was control.

Almost.

He ran a diagnostic.

This time, the signal held.

Clean.

Continuous.

Reliable, at least for now.

Ryan leaned back slightly, shoulders easing by a fraction. One problem resolved. A thousand are still waiting.

That was the nature of it.

Systems didn't fail all at once. They failed in layers, in whispers, in small betrayals that accumulated until something finally broke loud enough to be noticed.

His job wasn't to stop failure.

It was to stay ahead of it.

He glanced toward the pressure tanks lining the wall, their surfaces worn, valves marked with handwritten notes layered over older, faded labels. Each one contained a margin of survival measured in hours.

Out here, pressure was everything.

Lose it, and nothing else mattered.

He wiped his hands on a cloth that was already too dirty to make a difference and reached for the next component without hesitation.

The in-between was over.

Now there was work again.

And work, at least, made sense.

CHAPTER TWENTY-FOUR

QUIET CALCULATIONS

The stars beyond the viewport looked still.

They were not.

Ryan knew that. Every point of light was moving, falling, drifting through gravitational wells and invisible vectors that never truly stopped. Motion everywhere. Constant. Relentless.

But through the thick glass, framed by the scratched metal of the cockpit, it all looked calm.

Deceptively calm.

He sat hunched forward, one elbow on his knee, gloved fingers pressed lightly against his temple. The gesture wasn't dramatic. It was functional. Pressure against pressure, something to hold the thoughts in place.

They kept slipping anyway.

The next job.

It circled his mind the same way the counterweight circled the ship, predictable, unavoidable, and dangerous if misjudged.

A luxury liner.

That meant money.

It also meant complexity. Systems layered on systems. Redundancies hide failures. Wealth attracts risk.

And people.

Too many variables.

Ryan exhaled slowly, eyes drifting to the instruments in front of him, static readings. Stable numbers. Everything within tolerance.

For now.

He tried to run the job in his head the way he ran diagnostics.

Inputs. Conditions. Failure points.

The moment he stepped outside the ship, everything changed.

Out there, space wasn't empty. It was hostile precision. Cold that stripped heat faster than the body could react. Micrometeoroids are moving faster than thought. Surfaces that cut, tore, and failed without warning.

And the silence.

That was the part he didn't quantify.

The last time, he had hesitated.

Just a fraction.

Just enough.

His body had locked, muscles refusing instruction, mind splitting between action and fear. Systems still worked. Training still existed. But something deeper had stalled.

He had forced through it.

Barely.

Ryan's jaw tightened.

He had not told Jennifer.

She would adjust. Compensate. She takes on more risk herself to cover his hesitation. She always did.

That wasn't acceptable.

He shifted slightly in his seat, the suit creaking softly as the internal frame adjusted with him. The repair he had just completed held steady. No alerts. No warnings.

At least one variable was under control.

Money.

That was the anchor.

Everything else drifted, but money pinned reality into something measurable. Fuel costs. Parts. Consumables. Transmission fees. Time.

Time was the worst of it.

Every delay costs.

Every mistake compounded.

He thought of Sedna.

Distance is measured not just in kilometers, but in delay. In the hours between messages. In the long, stretched thread of responsibility that never slackened.

His parents.

Waiting without saying it.

Needing without asking.

Ryan pressed his fingers harder against his temple, then let his hand fall.

The fear didn't disappear.

It settled.

Compressed into something smaller. Denser. Usable.

Like pressure in a tank.

He leaned forward and keyed the console, pulling up the job data again. Schematics flickered into view, layered and complex. Hull sections. Access points. Structural stress lines from the asteroid impact.

A puzzle.

A dangerous one.

But still a puzzle.

And puzzles could be solved.

Ryan's gaze sharpened as he began isolating sections, marking likely failure zones, tracing pathways through the structure where a human could move without becoming another piece of debris.

One good job.

That was all it took.

He straightened slightly, the hesitation from earlier now buried beneath calculation.

Outside, the stars remained still.

CHAPTER TWENTY-FIVE

FIRST TO THE WOUND

The liner filled the viewport like a broken city.

Two massive hulls, once polished for the wealthy, now scarred and torn where the asteroid had punched through. Metal peeled outward in jagged petals. Debris drifted in slow halos around the impact site, each fragment tracing silent arcs through the vacuum.

Damage was never clean.

It always spread.

Ryan did not look at the spectacle for long. His eyes moved past the obvious destruction, searching for structure beneath it. Load paths. Stress fractures are secondary failures waiting to cascade.

Where something broke mattered more than how it looked.

Jennifer leaned forward slightly in her chair, hands moving with quiet precision across the controls. Her posture was relaxed, but the ship responded instantly to every input, adjusting position in small, controlled bursts.

She had already solved the approach.

Ryan had not even noticed when she did it.

“Whoa, looks like the asteroid really clocked it one,” she said, voice light, almost impressed.

Ryan said nothing at first.

He had already seen something else.

Movement.

His gaze narrowed, tracking a shape tucked near the damaged section of the liner. A ship. Smaller. Closer than it should be.

Too close.

He exhaled once, slowly.

“Oh no,” he said, more to himself than to her. “Barich is here already.”

The name settled into the space between them.

Jennifer’s hands did not pause. If anything, her movements became slightly sharper, more efficient.

Of course, he was here.

First on-site gets paid.

Everyone else gets nothing.

Ryan felt the calculation snap into place. Time collapsed. Options narrowed.

The job was no longer just dangerous.

It was competitive.

Jennifer glanced toward him, her expression unchanged, but her tone shifted, clean, direct, leaving no space for hesitation.

“Ok, get down there and patch the hole before Barich steals our thunder.”

Ryan looked back out at the torn hull.

At the drifting debris.

At the narrow margins where a human body could move without being shredded or lost.

The fear was still there.

But now it had somewhere to go.

He stood.

The motion was deliberate, controlled. No wasted energy. No visible hesitation. The suit adjusted around him, systems syncing as he moved toward the airlock.

Inside, his thoughts aligned into sequence.

Entry point.

Anchor.

Path.

Repair.

Exit.

No space for anything else.

Behind him, Bessy held steady under Jennifer's control, engines whispering corrections that kept them in perfect relation to the drifting wreck.

Ahead, the liner waited.

And somewhere out there, Barich was already moving.

Ryan reached the airlock and placed his hand on the control.

First on-site gets paid.

Ryan cycled the door.

CHAPTER TWENTY-SIX

CROSSING THE THRESHOLD

The door would not open.

Ryan felt it in the mechanism first. Resistance in the seals. Strain in the hinges. The airlock had held pressure too long, and now it gave it up reluctantly.

A thin gap formed.

Gas vented hard.

White streams tore past him, vanishing instantly into a vacuum as the pressure equalized. The sound was brief. Sharp.

Silence replaced it.

Absolute.

The door continued to grind open until the aperture cleared.

Beyond it, nothing.

No glass.

No barrier.

Just space.

Ryan stepped forward into the airlock chamber as the last of the atmosphere escaped. His suit compensated automatically, systems stabilizing, pressure holding firm.

He did not look outside yet.

First, he checked himself.

Seal integrity.

Oxygen flow.

Thermal balance.

All green.

He engaged his mag boots.

A soft pull locked him to the deck.

Control.

Only then did he move to the edge of the open airlock.

He stopped just short of stepping out.

CHAPTER TWENTY-SEVEN

THE OPEN THRESHOLD

There was no window.

The airlock door was open.

Ryan stood at the edge of it, looking directly out into space.

Nothing separated him from the void.

The damaged luxury liner hung below him, vast and torn open. Metal curled outward from the impact. Debris drifted in slow, lethal arcs.

A fearful sight. Full of dangers.

Depth broke apart.

Distance became meaningless.

The liner felt both near and unreachable at once.

Vertigo surged.

Ryan felt it rise in his chest, tightening, pressing, and threatening to stall him where he stood.

His boots held.

His body did not believe it.

There was no ground.

No horizon.

Only open space.

Only fall without falling.

He forced his vision to narrow.

Edges. Motion. Structure.

The wreck resolved into pathways.

The debris into vectors.

The void into measurable space.

His breathing steadied.

The fear remained.

Compressed.

Contained.

Useful.

Ryan leaned forward.

A small movement.

A commitment.

CHAPTER TWENTY-EIGHT

LOCK

The void took him.

His body remained anchored to the edge of the airlock, boots locked, suit stable, and systems nominal.

But everything else.

Stopped.

The liner filled his vision.

Too large.

Too open.

Too wrong.

Distance collapsed into something meaningless. The structure lost shape, becoming fragments, edges, motion without pattern. Debris drifted through it in slow arcs that didn't resolve into anything predictable.

Ryan didn't step forward.

Didn't step back.

His hand rested on the frame.

Unmoving.

Inside his helmet, the HUD continued to update.

Vectors.

Safe paths.

Collision warnings.

All correct.

All useless.

Command and action had separated.

A fault.

His breathing echoed in the helmet.

Too loud.

Too fast.

The system compensated.

He didn't.

"Ryan," Jennifer said.

Her voice cut through clean.

Precise.

“You’ve stopped.”

He didn’t answer.

Couldn’t.

The liner rotated slightly.

A section of hull peeled past his field of view, revealing a deeper fracture and an opening large enough to take him in, swallow him whole.

His vision narrowed.

The edges dimmed.

Focus collapsed inward.

Unsafe.

The word didn’t form in language.

It existed as certainty.

“Ryan,” Jennifer said again, sharper now. “You need to move.”

Nothing.

The HUD flickered.

A new element cut across the display.

Red.

A vector.

Closing.

Ryan didn't process it.

"Barich is accelerating," Jennifer said. "You have less than two minutes."

That reached him.

Time.

A constraint.

The number appeared in his vision.

1:52

Counting down.

Ryan's fingers tightened slightly against the frame.

Movement.

Small.

Insufficient.

The void pressed in.

Too much space.

Too many variables.

No ground.

No reference.

No control.

The system in his mind tried to resolve it.

Failed.

Looped.

“Listen to me,” Jennifer said.

Different tone now.

Lower.

More direct.

Ryan’s breathing hitched.

Still too fast.

Still too loud.

“Just one movement,” she said. “That’s it.”

The countdown continued.

1:31

Debris crossed his path.

One fragment drifted close.

Too close.

The HUD flared.

Warning.

Ryan didn't react.

Didn't move.

The fragment passed.

Missed.

Barely.

"Ryan!" Jennifer snapped. "That one hits, and you're done. Move!"

The words hit harder.

Ryan closed his eyes.

Just for a fraction of a second.

The liner disappeared.

The noise dimmed.

He reduced it.

One step.

His grip tightened.

His foot disengaged.

A soft click.

Final.

For a fraction of a second.

Nothing held him.

The void waited.

Small.

Enough.

He drifted forward.

The HUD recalibrated instantly.

Path lines reformed.

The system returned.

Because he had re-entered it.

“Good,” Jennifer said immediately. “Keep that. Don’t stop.”

The countdown ticked.

1:08

Ryan’s breathing steadied.

He adjusted.

A small correction.

The projected path shifted.

Clean.

Predictable.

Real.

The liner resolved again.

Entry point.

Distance.

Timing.

“Ryan,” Jennifer said, controlled again now, “he’s still closing.”

Ryan didn’t look back.

Didn’t need to.

He could feel it.

Pressure from behind.

Time collapsing.

It focused him.

He exhaled slowly.

And moved again.

This time.

On purpose.

CHAPTER TWENTY-NINE

PRESSURE

Her voice cut through the silence, sharp, precise, controlled.

“You were the one who told us to come, Ryan. What do you mean you can’t move?”

The liner filled his vision.

Exposure. Something too large to be reduced into parts.

His hand stayed locked on the frame.

He didn’t answer.

Inside the ship, Jennifer sat surrounded by systems that obeyed her. Inputs produced outputs. Noise became signal. Chaos became manageable.

Out here, there was no such translation.

Only raw input.

Only consequence.

“We need this money,” she said. “Snap out of it.”

The words landed. He understood them. Filed them. Knew exactly where they fit in the system.

But understanding didn't produce motion.

The HUD continued to update across his vision, clean, precise, and relentless.

Vectors.
Safe paths.
Collision probabilities.

All correct.

All unusable.

Command and action had separated.

A fault condition.

Ryan's breathing echoed inside the helmet, too loud, too fast, each inhale feeding the next before it could settle. The sound filled the space, crowding out everything else.

"Barich is going to take the contract," Jennifer said.

That reached deeper.

Loss of contract: no revenue, no repair, no return to work.

System failure.

He closed his eyes for a fraction of a second.

The liner disappeared.

The noise dimmed.

Just the load.

Too many variables.

Too much space.

No reference point.

His mind kept trying to solve the entire system at once, only to fail.

Looping.

“Listen to me,” Jennifer said.

Different tone now.

Lower. Direct.

“You don’t need the whole path.”

His breathing hitched.

“You only need the next movement.”

The words didn’t inspire him.

They constrained the problem.

Reduced it.

That he could work with.

The countdown flickered into focus.

A fragment drifted across his path, slow, silent, and inevitable. The HUD flared red, projecting impact timing, trajectory, and consequence.

Ryan didn’t move.

The fragment passed.

Missed him by less than a meter.

He closed his eyes again just long enough to cut the noise.

Just the excess.

One movement.

That was all.

His grip tightened.

He disengaged his boot.

A soft click echoed through the suit.

For a fraction of a second, nothing held him.

No structure.

No stability.

No correction.

He fired the thrusters.

A short burst.

Deliberate.

Just enough to change state.

He drifted forward.

Unstable. Slightly off-axis. Imperfect.

But moving.

The HUD responded instantly.

Solutions reappeared.

The projected path shifted.

Cleaner.

Predictable.

The liner resolved again not as chaos, but as structure.

Entry point. Distance. Timing.

“Ryan,” Jennifer said, steady now, “he’s still closing.”

He didn’t look back.

Didn’t need to.

He could feel it.

Time compressing. Options narrowing. Pressure is increasing from behind.

But it didn’t freeze him anymore.

It focused him.

He adjusted his trajectory again, deliberately this time, not reactively.

The line held.

For the first time since stepping out into the void, his movement matched his intent.

He exhaled slowly.

CHAPTER THIRTY

IMPACT VELOCITY

Her restraint broke.

“Get out there, you big baby!”

The words slammed into Ryan’s helmet, raw and unfiltered. No precision now. No measured tone. Just force.

Jennifer was shouting.

Someone cornered.

“Don’t you understand?” she demanded. “We need this money.”

The systems around her continued their quiet, obedient work. Screens updated. Trajectories refined. Warnings pulsed in soft, insistent rhythms.

None of it mattered.

Not compared to the human variable.

Ryan.

“You know I can’t go,” she said, the anger sharpening into something more dangerous. “So it has to be you.”

That was the equation.

Simple.

Unavoidable.

She could fly the ship.

He could leave it.

There was no redundancy for courage.

"Listen," she pushed, faster now, as if speed alone could force motion. "Just go. Forget about everything and just go!"

The command hung in the void between them.

Ryan opened his eyes.

The liner was still there.

Closer now.

Or maybe it only felt that way.

Fragments of hull drifted past the airlock opening, spinning slowly, catching light that had travelled millions of kilometers just to illuminate wreckage.

A section of the ship peeled away in silence.

No sound.

But he imagined it anyway.

Felt it.

His breathing echoed inside his helmet.

Too loud.

Too fast.

Jennifer's voice lingered, reverberating through him, colliding with everything else already there.

Fear.

Obligation.

Memory.

He thought of Sedna.

Of distance measured not just in kilometers, but in time. In delay. In isolation.

Of people waiting.

Of systems that did not care if he failed.

Of contracts that did not forgive hesitation.

He looked down.

His hand.

Still on the frame.

Still gripping.

But no longer frozen.

A tremor moved through it.

Small.

Controlled.

Movement.

He shifted his weight forward.

Barely.

But enough.

The airlock threshold was a memory.

It was a line.

CHAPTER THIRTY-ONE

CROSSING THE LINE

"Ok, I am on route," Ryan said.

The words sounded smaller than the moment.

Flattened by the comms.

Reduced.

But real.

His boot hovered, suspended. Outside. Safety and exposure. Thought and action.

Then it settled.

Contact.

And everything.

The void did not resist him. It did not push back. It simply accepted his presence without acknowledgment, as if he were just another fragment drifting free of something larger.

Images surged through his mind.

Fragments.

His parents are on Sedna. The quiet rooms. The slow pace of age. The unspoken reliance on money that arrived late, or not at all.

Jennifer, younger, laughing at something reckless, already unafraid of motion.

The ship.

Bessy.

Held together by patches, by persistence, by necessity.

One step, then the next. But there were no steps. He was floating.

He forced the sequence.

Expanding infinity pressing against his vision from every direction.

Just the next movement.

His second foot lifted.

Followed.

Committed.

Ryan tried to narrow the world.

Reduce it.

Frame by frame.

Handhold.

Step.

Anchor point.

But the scale kept bleeding through.

The liner stretched across his vision, impossibly large, broken open like something that should never have failed.

Debris moved slowly, but with the quiet certainty of lethal velocity.

There was no up.

No down.

Only vectors.

“I’m going now, Jennifer,” he said.

The words came out softer than he intended.

Something closer to surrender.

Or acceptance.

Behind him, the airlock remained open.

Ahead of him, the job waited.

Between the two, Ryan moved.

Finally.

CHAPTER THIRTY-TWO

MOMENTUM

Shaking.

Enough that every movement required intention.

Ryan gripped the handle of the tool crate and pushed.

Slowly.

Deliberately.

The box resisted at first, inertia holding it in place as if the ship itself did not want to let go. Then, with a subtle shift, it broke free.

Floating.

Weightless.

But not harmless.

Mass remained.

Momentum waited.

The crate drifted outward, its edges catching faint light, its surface scarred from years of use. Tools inside shifted with dull, muted thuds he could feel more than hear through his gloves.

Ryan kept one hand on it.

Guiding.

Controlling.

Because once it got away from him, it would not stop.

Beyond it, the luxury liner hung in pieces.

Closer now.

The word LUXURY is still visible along its broken hull, absurd in its persistence.

Fragments of debris drifted between him and the target, slow-moving hazards that demanded constant awareness.

Ryan exhaled.

Forced it steadily.

This was different.

This was work.

Something he understood.

Move the crate.

Keep control.

Don't lose it.

His boots adjusted against, small corrections, anchoring him as he extended further into the void.

The crate continued forward.

And with it, Ryan followed.

Working.

One controlled motion at a time.

CHAPTER THIRTY-THREE

OUTSIDE THE MACHINE

The tether held.

A thin line.

Insignificant against the scale of space.

But absolute.

Ryan drifted just beyond the hull of Bessy, the ship looming beside him like something alive but tired. Scars ran along her surface, patched plates, and mismatched panels, burn marks layered over older burn marks.

History written in damage.

His boots no longer touched anything.

No frame.

No edge.

No inside.

Only the tether connected him back to something that counted as safe.

He didn't look at it.

Didn't need to.

He could feel it.

A quiet pull at his waist, a constant reminder that he was not entirely alone out here.

The stars were sharper now.

Present.

Every direction was open.

Every direction was wrong.

Ryan forced his attention back to the ship.

Bessy.

Close.

Concrete.

Manageable.

Her airlock door remained open behind him, a warm rectangle of light cutting into the black. Inside, systems hummed, air existed, structure held.

Out here, none of that mattered.

Only motion.

Only control.

His gloved hand reached out, finding the hull. Metal under-pressure suit. Familiar. Solid. Real.

He held onto it.

Anchored.

The tool crate moved ahead of him, slow and obedient now under his guidance, drifting toward the damaged liner in the distance.

That was the job.

The job.

Ryan adjusted his grip and pulled himself along the hull in small, deliberate movements. Each action is calculated. Each shift is controlled.

Behind him, Bessy's engines glowed faintly, a low burn maintaining position, keeping the geometry of the operation intact.

Ahead, the liner waited.

Broken.

Silent.

Full of money.

Ryan swallowed.

The sound was loud inside his helmet.

Then he moved again.

CHAPTER THIRTY-FOUR

CUT LOOSE

"Ok, Jennifer… disconnecting the tether now."

Ryan's voice wavered despite his effort to steady it.

The line at his waist tugged gently, a quiet, persistent reminder of everything behind him. Safety. Air. Structure. Return.

Home, in the smallest possible sense.

He didn't look back.

Looking back would make it harder.

"Making my way to the luxury liner," he added.

There was a pause.

His hand moved to the tether release.

A simple mechanism.

Engineered for reliability.

No ambiguity.

One action.

Permanent consequence.

He hesitated.

The system in his mind tried to calculate outcomes, probabilities, vectors of risk. Too many variables. Too much uncertainty.

No solution.

Only decision.

He triggered the release.

The tether snapped free.

It simply drifted away, curling slowly into the void, no longer connected to anything that cared about him.

Ryan was alone.

Completely.

The silence deepened.

Or maybe he only noticed it now.

He commanded the suit.

Thrusters engaged with a soft vibration through his body, a controlled push that translated intent into motion.

Light flared behind his boots.

Small corrections.

The crate moved with him, guided by his grip, its mass now something he had to account for constantly. Every adjustment mattered. Every impulse had a consequence.

Ahead, the liner grew.

Details sharpened.

Torn plating. Exposed framework. Dark openings where structure had failed.

A wound.

Waiting.

“There’s still a chance,” he muttered, more to himself than to Jennifer.

A slim one.

But real.

Barich would be coming.

Fast.

Aggressive.

Confident.

Ryan adjusted his trajectory, threading between drifting debris, trusting the suit's calculations while fighting the instinct to overcorrect.

Too much input would kill him.

Precision mattered more than speed.

The distance closed.

And for the first time since stepping out of the airlock, Ryan was no longer thinking about going back.

Only forward.

CHAPTER THIRTY-FIVE

THE RACE GEOMETRY (HUD)

Now he could see it.

The liner drifted at the center of everything, a broken mass still carrying momentum from whatever had torn it apart. Around it, debris traced slow, deadly arcs, each fragment following its own path, predictable in isolation, chaotic in total.

But Ryan no longer saw it with his eyes alone.

His helmet came alive.

A faint grid settled over the void, barely visible, just enough to give shape to nothing. Lines appeared clean and precise, cutting through the chaos.

The liner was outlined in amber.

Its hull flickered where damage had compromised its integrity. A section near the midline pulsed red and opened, jagged but viable. A rotating marker locked onto it.

ENTRY POINT

Ryan focused on it.

The rest dimmed slightly.

Barich's ship appeared next.

Not as a shape.

As a threat.

A sharp red vector curved toward the liner, tighter than his own path, more aggressive. Numbers flickered beside it, updating constantly.

Distance.

Closing speed.

Time.

INTERCEPT RISK

Ryan didn't need the label.

He felt it anyway.

Behind him, Bessy glowed in soft blue.

A single anchor point in the darkness.

Stable.

Patient.

Home reduced to a marker and a direction.

His own path stretched out ahead, a thin blue line projected from his chest, bending slightly as the system recalculated with each micro-adjustment of his thrusters.

He nudged left.

The line shifted.

Instantly.

Debris lit up around him.

Most of it is yellow.

Safe.

One fragment ahead flared red.

A number appeared beside it.

2.8s.

Ryan adjusted.

A small burst.

The line curved.

The warning vanished.

Precision.

Numbers crawled along the edges of his vision.

Oxygen.

Pressure.

Fuel.

He ignored them.

"Jennifer," he said, steadier now, "I see him."

His eyes tracked the red vector again.

Barich was cutting corners.

Taking a risk Ryan couldn't afford.

Ryan leaned into the system.

He selected a narrower corridor barely visible between drifting fragments. The HUD confirmed it with a faint green overlay.

VIABLE PATH

Margins tight.

No room for error.

He increased thrust.

Carefully.

Too much and the crate would drift.

Too little and Barich would win.

The blue line extended.

Locked.

Committed.

The liner grew larger, its torn hull no longer abstract but immediate, detailed, reachable.

The red vector tightened.

Closing.

Ryan's path cut between them.

A third line.

Fragile.

Human.

But guided now.

By data.

By a system that turned infinity into something he could survive.

If he trusted it.

If he didn't hesitate.

"Warning indicators flooded Ryan's vision."

Radiation climbing.

Temperature rising.

Debris density is increasing.

Each alert pulsed against his focus, demanding attention he could not spare.

The path narrowed.

The margin for error vanished.

Barich was closing fast.

Ryan forced his breathing steady.

One line. One path.

Follow it or die."

CHAPTER THIRTY-SIX

THE WELD

Ryan's world narrowed to the seam.

The rest of the liner, its torn architecture, the drifting debris, the distant red arc of Barich's approach, fell away as he brought the tool up and fixed his attention on the jagged edge of the ruptured hull in front of him.

Metal curled outward like something peeled open by force rather than cut. The edges were uneven, crystalline in places where microscopic stress had fractured the structure. It caught the light in dull, broken reflections that shifted as the wreck rotated.

He anchored himself.

Left hand to a surviving rib of structure just inside the breach. Boots magnetized, though the pull was inconsistent along the warped surface. The crate hovered at his side, tethered now by his grip alone, mass a quiet threat waiting for a mistake.

Ryan positioned the welding tool.

A small thing, compact, scarred from use. It hummed faintly as it came online, a vibration that travelled through his glove and into his wrist.

He didn't rush.

Couldn’t.

The hull wasn’t stable. The liner’s slow rotation introduced a constant drift to everything. Even anchored, he could feel it as a subtle lateral pull that shifted the seam away from him by millimeters at a time.

He compensated.

Adjusted his stance.

Brought the tool closer.

The first arc struck.

Light bloomed.

Harsh. White. Immediate.

It burned against his visor, scattering reflections across the inside of his helmet as the heat intensified. The HUD dimmed automatically, filtering intensity, but the flare still dominated his vision for a fraction of a second.

Then it settled.

A controlled point of energy.

The metal responded reluctantly.

Edges softened.

Flowed.

Ryan moved the tool slowly along the seam, guiding molten material into the gaps where vacuum had torn it apart. The motion required precision more than strength. Too fast, and the bond would be weak. Too slow and the heat would spread, warping what remained of the structure.

He tracked it as much by feel as by sight.

Resistance through the glove.

Subtle changes in vibration.

The way the arc behaved as it met different densities in the fractured hull.

Behind it all, his breathing.

Steady.

Forced.

The HUD flickered at the edges of his vision.

Radiation levels are rising.

Temperature gradients are shifting.

Debris vectors updating.

He ignored them.

The seam mattered more.

If he could close it, he might even restore partial integrity. The liner would hold pressure long enough to stabilize systems inside. Long enough to claim the job.

Long enough to get paid.

A fragment drifted past his peripheral vision.

Too close.

The HUD marked it red for an instant.

Ryan didn't look.

Didn't break the arc.

He trusted the trajectory.

Trusted the calculation.

The fragment passed.

The warning vanished.

His hand remained steady.

The weld line grew.

A thin, glowing path sealing fracture to fracture, turning chaos into continuity, one controlled movement at a time.

He shifted position slightly, boots releasing and re-engaging with a muted click as he adjusted his angle. The liner rotated beneath him, slow but constant, forcing him to chase the seam as it moved.

That was the only way.

“Status?” Jennifer’s voice came through, quieter now, controlled again.

Ryan didn’t answer immediately.

He finished the current section, drawing the arc to a clean stop before pulling the tool back.

The metal cooled in seconds, the glow fading to dull grey.

“Holding,” he said.

But holding.

He repositioned.

The next section was worse.

The fracture widened, edges misaligned, and the original structure twisted just enough to resist closure. He would need to build material here, not just seal it.

More time.

Time he didn't have.

Barich's vector pulsed at the edge of his vision.

Closer.

Ryan exhaled slowly.

Then began again.

The arc flared.

Brighter this time against the deeper gap.

He layered material carefully, building a bridge across absence, each pass reinforcing the last. The tool vibrated more forcefully under the increased load, a subtle instability that travelled up his arm.

He compensated.

Adjusted pressure.

Slowed the pass.

The seam began to take shape.

The liner shifted again beneath him, rotation bringing a new angle, a new drift.

Ryan leaned into it, following the motion rather than resisting, his body aligning with the structure as if he were part of it.

For a moment, the fear disappeared.

There was only the work.

The seam.

The arc of light cutting through darkness.

He completed the section and pulled back.

Paused.

Checked.

The HUD has been updated.

Hull integrity: partial.

Pressure retention: possible.

It was enough.

Ryan moved to the next segment without hesitation.

Behind him, space remained vast and indifferent.

Ahead of him, the liner still bled vacuum through wounds too large to ignore.

And somewhere out there, Barich was still coming.

Ryan lowered the tool and struck the arc again.

Because stopping now would mean losing everything.

CHAPTER THIRTY-SEVEN

BARICH

The hull tilted under him again.

Ryan adjusted without thinking, boots re-locking against a new plane as the liner's slow rotation shifted the angle of pull across his body. Nothing stayed consistent long enough to trust. Not even the surface beneath his hands.

He pressed closer to the metal, reducing his profile against something that didn't care if he stayed attached or not.

The seam ran upward, no longer a clean fracture but a spreading network of stress that refused to resolve into anything simple. It branched, split, rejoined. Each line carried force from deeper inside the ship toward the surface, where he was trying to hold it together.

He followed the worst of it.

His glove traced the line.

A faint tremor beneath the material.

Subtle.

Persistent.

“That’s the one,” he murmured.

The tool came up.

He aligned it with the direction of stress, not the visible break. The weld had to oppose the force, not just cover the damage.

He struck the arc.

Light flared across the hull, scattering in sharp reflections that fractured across his visor. The HUD dimmed automatically, compensating, but the brightness still cut through his focus before settling.

He moved with it.

Slow.

Deliberate.

The metal resisted, not refusing, but unstable. Shifting under the heat. Pulling away from the shape he was trying to impose.

He adjusted.

Pressure.

Angle.

Speed.

Feeding material into the seam in controlled increments.

For a moment, it held.

The HUD has been updated.

Integrity: marginal.
Spread: slowed.

Not fixed.

But contained.

Ryan pulled back slightly, just enough to assess.

The structure didn't respond the way it should have.

The stress didn't dissipate.

It redistributed.

The seam thickened where he had reinforced it, but further up, new fractures began to form, branching away from the weld line as if the force had simply found another path.

That wasn't normal.

"You're seeing that," he said.

A brief delay.

“Yes,” Jennifer replied.

Too brief.

The liner shuddered.

Stronger this time.

Ryan killed the arc instantly, holding position as the vibration passed through the structure and into his body. It wasn’t a single movement; it layered, internal shifts translating outward, distorting the hull by degrees.

He waited.

One breath.

Then another.

The motion settled.

But the pattern had changed.

“Jennifer,” he said, voice tighter now, “this isn’t local.”

A pause.

Processing.

“Define.”

“Stress propagation,” he said. “It’s moving.”

He looked up the slope of torn metal.

The central rupture loomed above him, a chaotic break where the asteroid had punched through, forcing the structure outward. Layers peeled back under pressure too fast to contain.

Everything was still redistributing from that point.

And now

It wasn’t stabilizing.

It was adapting.

“Expected,” Jennifer said. “You are near the impact zone.”

“No,” Ryan said.

Flat.

Immediate.

“This is different.”

The seam beneath his hand shifted.

Not visually.

Physically.

A subtle realignment that didn't match any external force.

Ryan didn't like that.

He reignited the arc.

This time, he worked faster.

Precision wasn't enough anymore.

He reinforced aggressively, bridging sections that no longer aligned cleanly. The weld built up in uneven ridges, holding just enough to resist the spreading fracture.

The liner answered with another shudder.

Closer.

More violent.

A fragment drifted past his shoulder.

Too close.

The HUD flagged it.

Ryan ignored it.

The seam mattered more.

His left hand shifted forward.

Searching.

Found purchase.

Sharp.

Unstable but usable.

His arms began to ache.

From holding precision under conditions that refused to allow it.

The arc flickered.

He corrected.

Maintained.

Kept moving.

The liner rotated again, exposing deeper layers of the rupture: collapsed decks, twisted corridors, and the internal structure forced outward into shapes never meant for load.

A system breaking past design limits.

Barich would be targeting cleaner access.

Faster routes.

Ryan didn't have that option.

He was already committed here.

He finished another section and pulled back.

The HUD has been updated.

Integrity: marginal.
Spread: slowed.

Still failing.

Just slower.

The hull was still trying to tear itself apart.

Ryan was the only option to delay the collapse.

CHAPTER THIRTY-EIGHT

MISSILE

The warning did not begin as sound.

It began as an intrusion.

Ryan was still leaning into the weld, the arc steady in his hand, the seam narrowing under controlled heat, when something cut across his vision that did not belong to the work. A color. A pulse. Sharp enough to override everything else.

Red.

It flooded the edges of his HUD, then surged inward, replacing data with urgency.

For a fraction of a second, he didn't react.

His hand continued its motion, finishing the line he had already committed to, because stopping mid-pass would weaken the bond. The arc dragged to completion before he pulled the tool away.

Then the world snapped back in.

The warnings resolved.

Vector lines.

Closing speed.

Impact prediction.

Ryan froze.

The information didn't make sense at first. It existed as raw data numbers, trajectories, and probabilities without context that his mind could immediately place.

Incoming.

His nerves returned.

He lifted his head.

The seam disappeared from relevance.

The liner fell away.

The void reassembled itself around him with sudden, brutal clarity.

A streak through the debris field.

Moving with intent.

Fast.

Too fast.

Ryan's eyes struggled to track it, the object resolving only in fragments between the clutter of rock and metal that filled the space around the liner. It flared briefly as it crossed a gap, heat, propulsion, controlled motion, cutting through randomness.

A missile.

The word formed without resistance.

Clean.

Final.

His body still hadn't moved.

The HUD screamed at him now, warnings stacking over each other, flooding his vision with paths and projections that all ended the same way.

Impact.

Ryan exhaled.

A single, controlled breath.

Then everything narrowed.

The vastness collapsed.

The debris field was reduced to vectors.

The liner to a surface he could use.

The missile is on a line.

He disengaged one boot.

The magnetic lock released with a dull internal click that he felt more than heard.

His body shifted immediately, the change in constraint translating into motion as the weak artificial pull from the liner dragged him sideways across the hull.

He didn't fight it.

He used it.

A push from his left hand.

A small burst from his thrusters.

The movement was not fast.

It didn't need to be.

It needed to be correct.

The missile adjusted.

Ryan saw destruction in the way the vector line curved.

Tracking.

Guided.

His jaw tightened.

He pushed harder.

Another burst.

The crate lagged behind him, its mass resisting the change in direction before it followed, pulling against his grip and threatening to destabilize his trajectory.

He let it go.

The release was immediate.

The crate drifted free, continuing along his previous path, a ghost of where he had been.

Ryan shifted again.

Changed angle.

Reduced profile against the hull.

The missile's path split.

A fraction.

Then corrected.

Still tracking.

Too close now.

The time-to-impact collapsed into numbers too small to ignore.

Ryan saw the seam he had just welded.

A reinforced section.

Thicker.

Stronger.

He made the decision without thinking.

He drove himself toward it.

Boots re-engaged.

Hard.

Magnetic locks snapped into place as he slammed against the hull, flattening himself against the reinforced line he had created moments earlier.

The missile closed.

The world was reduced to a single line of motion converging on his position.

Ryan didn't look away.

Didn't blink.

The impact came.

A violent transmission through the hull, a shockwave that travelled through metal into his body, slamming through his arms, his chest, his helmet. The reinforced section barely absorbed and redistributed the energy along the weld line he had built.

The liner buckled.

A deep structural shudder rippled outward from the point of impact, distorting the geometry beneath him.

Ryan held.

Every muscle locked.

Every contact point engaged.

The hull tried to throw him free.

He refused.

The shock passed.

Fragments exploded outward from the impact site, debris accelerating into new trajectories, turning the surrounding space into something sharper, more lethal.

Ryan remained pressed against the hull.

Breathing.

Controlled.

But tighter now.

The HUD flickered, recalculating.

New vectors.

New risks.

The missile was gone.

But its effect remained.

Ryan closed his eyes for a fraction of a second.

Then opened them again.

The seam was still there.

Damaged.

But holding.

He swallowed.

The sound was loud inside his helmet.

Then, quietly,

“Jennifer?”

CHAPTER THIRTY-NINE

HOLD OR LEAVE

The hull was still moving.

Ryan felt it in the way his hands had to keep correcting, in the way the reinforced seam beneath him no longer held a single shape but flexed through a narrow range of instability. The impact had changed something deeper than the surface.

He stayed pressed against it anyway.

Breathing.

Counting.

Waiting for the system to settle into something he could trust.

It didn't.

The comms snapped alive.

"That stupid Barich fired a missile!"

Jennifer's voice cut through him, sharp enough to feel physical.

Ryan's eyes flicked outward, instinctively searching the debris field for confirmation he already had. The patterns had changed. Trajectories diverged in new ways, fragments moving faster and less predictably.

The explosion hadn't hit the liner; it had hit Bessy.

It had rewritten the environment around it.

"Get back here," she pushed, the control in her tone collapsing into urgency. "Now."

Ryan didn't move.

His hand tightened against the hull.

The reflex to obey was there, clean, direct, and almost automatic. The ship was safe. Structure. Air that didn't have to be fought for.

The reinforced section had taken the impact, but not cleanly. Hairline fractures spider outward from the weld, faint but growing, the metal around it stressed beyond what his earlier repair had accounted for.

It would fail.

It would tear open again under the redistributed load, undoing everything he had just forced into place.

And Barich.

Ryan's jaw tightened.

Barich would still be out there.

Closer now.

Waiting for exactly that.

“Ryan,” Jennifer said again, sharper, “move.”

He exhaled slowly.

Forced the decision into sequence.

Always the next step.

The words came out steady, but quieter than her urgency demanded.

“What?”

“The seam’s compromised,” Ryan said, eyes tracking the spreading stress lines as they crept across the hull.

Another pause.

Shorter.

“That’s not your problem if you’re dead,” she snapped.

Ryan didn’t answer that.

Because she wasn’t wrong.

But she wasn’t complete either.

He shifted his weight slightly, testing the hold beneath his boots. The magnetic locks bit into uneven metal, holding, but not with the certainty he wanted.

The liner flexed again.

A deeper movement.

Something inside is giving way.

Ryan reacted instantly, flattening himself, redistributing his weight as the surface beneath him distorted by degrees.

The seam pulled.

Just enough to matter.

He saw it.

A fraction of separation along the edge he had just sealed.

Too close.

“Ryan!”

Jennifer’s voice broke again, louder now, stripped of control.

His hand moved without hesitation now, guided by something that had already made the decision before he could articulate it.

“Ryan, you don’t have thirty seconds,” Jennifer shot back.

He didn’t respond.

Because arguing would cost time.

The hull shuddered again.

Debris streaked past in tighter patterns now, faster, more dangerous. The HUD was filled with warnings he refused to read.

His arms burned.

His grip tightened.

Behind him, somewhere beyond the debris and the distortion, Bessy waited.

Ahead of him, the liner tried to tear itself apart.

Between the two, Ryan.

CHAPTER FORTY

WHEN HOME BECOMES TARGET

Ryan felt it before he understood it.

A distortion in the background.

His head lifted slightly, instinct pulling his attention outward past the immediate work, past the fractured hull, into the wider field where motion meant danger.

At first, nothing was resolved.

Just debris.

Asteroids drifting in slow, indifferent arcs.

The distant burn of engines.

He froze.

Bessy.

The image assembled too quickly, too cleanly.

Her silhouette sat where he expected it to be, offset against the debris field, holding position relative to the liner. Familiar. Worn. Real.

Then the fire registered.

A sharp bloom of light along her midsection.

Too bright.

Too violent.

Ryan’s breath caught.

The explosion didn’t sound.

It spread.

A burst of incandescent fragments tore outward from her hull, followed by a dark plume that expanded unnaturally in vacuum, particulate matter venting from systems that had just been opened to space.

“No.”

The word left him without thought.

His body reacted before his mind could catch up.

He shifted, boots unlocking as he twisted toward her, losing contact with the liner for a fraction of a second before snapping one foot back into place to stop the drift.

His hand slipped.

Recovered.

His gaze locked on Bessy.

Fire continued to crawl along her exterior, licking out from a ruptured section near the engine housing. Internal components were exposed, glowing where they shouldn't, venting gases that crystallized and dispersed into the void.

She was bleeding.

Ryan's nerves returned.

"Jennifer."

The comms crackled.

For a moment, nothing came back.

Just static.

Just absence.

"I see it."

Her voice.

Tighter than he had ever heard it.

Controlled.

But only just.

Ryan swallowed.

"What happened?"

He already knew.

But he needed to hear it.

Needed confirmation.

Barich.

The thought hit clean.

Cold.

Ryan’s jaw locked.

He looked back at Bessy.

At the torn section of the hull.

The way the fire pulsed outward in uneven bursts, each one marking another system failing, another layer of protection stripped away.

That was their ship.

Air.

Shelter.

Return.

If it went.

There was nowhere to go.

Ryan forced himself to breathe.

Slow.

Controlled.

Assess.

Don’t react.

He scanned her visually, tracking the damage.

The hit had been surgical.

Mid-hull breach.

Engine-adjacent.

Dangerous.

But not immediately fatal.

If it spreads.

If the pressure systems cascaded.

“Can you hold it?” he asked.

A pause.

“I’m isolating,” Jennifer said. “Compartmentalizing now.”

Translation.

She was cutting sections loose.

Sacrificing parts of the ship to save the rest.

Ryan closed his eyes for half a second.

Opened them again.

Bessy was still burning.

Still venting.

Still alive.

For now.

His grip tightened on the liner’s hull.

The seam beneath him flexed.

A reminder.

He was still here.

Still working.

Still committed.

Two problems.

Both critical.

Both time-sensitive.

Neither waiting.

Ryan’s mind split.

The ship.

He had abandoned the repair.

The liner failed.

No salvage.

No payment.

Nothing to fix, Bessy.

Bessy might not survive long enough for it to matter.

Jennifer’s voice cut back in.

“Ryan.”

Just his name.

No instruction.

No command.

He heard what she didn’t say.

Come back.

Now.

Ryan looked at Bessy.

Burning.

Breaking.

Home.

His nerves returned.

The decision didn't come cleanly.

It never did.

He forced it anyway.

"Hold it together," he said.

To her.

To the ship.

To himself.

CHAPTER FORTY-ONE

BREAKING POINT

The fire on Bessy didn’t stop.

Ryan couldn’t make it stop.

He stared at it longer than he should have, long enough for the shape of the damage to burn into him, long enough for the movement of the flames and venting gas to become something he could not ignore or rationalize away.

It was real.

It was happening.

And he was there.

His hand tightened against the hull.

“Jennifer!”

The name tore out of him, raw, uncontrolled, and louder than anything he had said since leaving the ship. It echoed back through the suit as a confined distortion, a reminder that even his voice had nowhere to go.

Static answered first.

A thin, jagged noise that scraped across the comms channel like something broken.

Ryan's breathing shortened.

"Oh my god," The words came fast now, tripping over each other as his mind tried to catch up with what his eyes were telling him. "What a complete."

He cut himself off, jaw tightening hard enough to hurt.

Barich.

There was no one else.

No random strike.

No accident.

This was deliberate.

"Jennifer, are you okay?"

The question fell into silence.

The kind that stretched just long enough to let everything he didn't want to think about slip in.

His grip slipped slightly.

He corrected it instantly, fingers digging harder into the torn metal, grounding himself in something physical, something immediate.

The hull flexed beneath him.

He barely noticed.

His attention had left the liner.

It was anchored now to Bessy.

To the fire.

To the absence of an answer.

“Jennifer,” he said again, quieter this time, but tighter, more dangerous. “Answer me.”

A crackle.

“I’m here.”

Her voice.

Strained.

Compressed.

Alive.

Ryan’s eyes closed for a fraction of a second.

Relief didn't come cleanly.

It never did.

It arrived tangled with everything else.

"What's your status?" he pushed.

A breath on the other end.

Then, controlled:

"Compartment three's gone. I sealed it. Fire's contained to the engine housing for now."

For now.

Ryan swallowed.

"Can you hold it?"

Another pause.

Shorter this time.

"I don't know."

Honest.

Too honest.

Ryan's jaw tightened again.

His mind ran the numbers whether he wanted it to or not.

Engine housing breach.

Structural compromise.

Loss of compartment integrity.

Cascading failure pathways.

Too many variables.

“Ryan,” Jennifer said, her voice sharpening again, urgency pushing back through control, “you need to get back here.”

He didn’t answer.

Because he couldn’t.

Slower now.

A chance of fixing Bessy.

Ryan’s nerves returned.

His breathing lost its rhythm.

For a moment, everything fractured.

The work.

The ship.

The distance between them.

Too many problems.

Too little time.

“Why does everything go wrong the second I step out that hatch?” he muttered, the words low, almost lost inside his helmet.

Of inevitability.

His hand trembled.

Just once.

He stilled it.

Forced it back under control.

Fear pressed in.

A weight that sat behind his ribs and refused to move.

Anger followed.

Cleaner.

Hotter.

Directed.

Barich had done this.

A person.

A choice.

Ryan inhaled slowly.

Held it.

Let it out.

The motion steadied him just enough.

“Listen to me,” Jennifer said, cutting through his spiral. “You come back now, we deal with this together. You stay out there, I might not have a ship left for you to come back to.”

The words landed hard.

Simple.

Binary.

Ryan looked at Bessy.

The fire was still burning along her side.

Then at the seam.

Still failing.

Still his responsibility.

He felt the distance between the two like a physical tear.

The truth settled in with a quiet finality.

Something would be lost.

The only question was which.

Ryan's fingers tightened one last time against the hull.

Then loosened.

Just enough.

A hesitation.

Balanced on the edge of a decision that would define everything that came after.

And for the first time since stepping out into the void.

Ryan felt alone.

CHAPTER FORTY-TWO

FAULT LINES

The fire changed shape.

Ryan watched it through the drifting debris, through the shifting angles of the liner's rotation, through the thin veil of particles that caught light and distorted distance. It no longer flared outward in sharp bursts. It thickened.

Dark.

Heavy.

Smoke where there should be none.

It bled from Bessy's midsection in slow, rolling plumes, expanding into the void like something alive, something refusing to dissipate cleanly. The brightness beneath it dimmed, not because the fire was gone, but because it had burrowed inward.

Deeper.

Worse.

Ryan felt afraid.

That wasn't surface damage anymore.

That was internal.

"Jennifer," he said, quieter now, but more controlled. "What just changed?"

A flicker of static.

Then her voice, tighter, focused on something he could not see.

"Hold on," she said. "I'm checking."

Ryan's eyes tracked the ship.

Every detail mattered now.

The rupture line.

The glow.

The way the plume expanded and then folded back on itself as it met colder space.

His mind built models whether he wanted it to or not.

Heat transfer.

Structural compromise.

Secondary ignition risk.

Too many pathways.

Too many ways this could cascade.

His body corrected automatically, hands tightening, boots adjusting against warped metal.

His attention remained fixed on Bessy.

“Jennifer.”

No answer.

Just the faint sound of her working keys, systems, the controlled chaos of someone trying to stay ahead of a problem that was already moving faster than it should.

Ryan swallowed.

The silence stretched.

“Okay,” she said.

The word came out.

Deliberate.

Too deliberate.

“I’m alive for now.”

Ryan exhaled, but the relief didn’t settle.

For now.

It never stayed contained.

"What's failing?" he asked.

"Engine housing took the worst of it," she replied. "I've isolated what I can. Some systems are offline. Others are thinking about it."

Thinking about it.

Ryan almost smiled.

Almost.

"Pressure?"

"Stable in the core sections," she said. "I've sealed the breach zones. Lost compartment three completely."

He pictured it.

He was concerned.

"Can you move?"

A pause.

Longer this time.

"I can," she said. "I shouldn't."

Translation.

The ship would respond.

But it might not survive the stress.

“Ryan,” Jennifer said, her voice shifting again, urgency pushing back through control. “You need to come back. Now.”

He didn’t answer.

Bessy is in the distance.

Work.

Home.

He felt the pull.

Tearing him down the middle.

“What an absolute tool,” Jennifer muttered suddenly, the anger cutting through her composure. “We are going to report him so hard.”

Ryan closed his eyes briefly.

To center.

Reporting Barich didn’t matter.

Consequences were a future problem.

Survival was immediate.

He opened his eyes again.

The ship.

He forced the equation into a simpler form.

Bessy might live.

Might.

Ryan inhaled slowly.

Held it.

Released it.

“Jennifer,” he said.

Her name carried more weight this time.

More decisions.

More finality.

“I hear you.”

“Then move,” she said.

No anger now.

Just urgency.

Ryan looked at Bessy one last time.

At the smoke.

At the damage.

At the ship that had carried him this far and might not carry him much further.

Ahead of him, the distance closed.

And everything that mattered waited on the other side of it.

CHAPTER FORTY-THREE

BURN AND RETURN

Bessy grew larger with every second.

Ryan drove himself forward with controlled bursts, the thrusters flaring hot against the cold vacuum, each pulse translating into forward motion that felt both urgent and painfully insufficient. The distance closed, but not fast enough to quiet the pressure building in his chest.

The damage sharpened as he approached.

What had been a distant wound resolved into detail, torn plating peeled back like ruptured skin, internal components exposed and blackened, sections still glowing with trapped heat. Smoke billowed outward in thick, slow rolls, particulate matter drifting and spreading, turning the space around the ship into a murky halo of debris and residue.

Bessy looked wrong.

Violated.

Ryan angled himself toward the hatch, adjusting his vector to avoid the worst of the drifting fragments. His HUD tracked collision paths, painting shifting corridors through the chaos. He threaded through them without hesitation, trusting the system just enough to keep moving.

The hull came up fast.

He cut thrust.

Drifted the last few meters.

Reached out.

His glove hit metal.

Solid.

Real.

He grabbed hold and pulled himself in, boots snapping against the surface with a magnetic bite that steadied him instantly. The ship's vibration travelled up through his legs, subtle and uneven, a system under strain but still alive.

“Jennifer, I’m at the hatch.”

“Get inside,” she said immediately.

No hesitation.

No excess words.

Ryan moved.

The hatch loomed open, its edges scorched but intact. He pulled himself through, dragging his body into the narrow entry space, sealing himself back inside the ship that now felt more fragile than ever.

The door cycled behind him.

Pressure equalized.

Air returned not something he needed to breathe through the suit, but something he felt all the same. Presence. Containment. Survival.

He didn't wait.

Helmet off.

Gloves loose.

Moving.

The interior smelled wrong.

Burnt.

Metallic.

The scent of systems pushed beyond design limits.

Ryan followed it instinctively, moving through tight corridors toward the control section where he knew Jennifer would be.

The lighting flickered.

He entered the cockpit.

Jennifer stood at the console, her posture rigid, movements precise as her hands moved across controls faster than he could track. The screen in front of her showed Bessy from the outside, a rotating feed that highlighted damage zones in stark overlays.

Ryan stepped in beside her.

Close enough to feel the tension in her movements.

Close enough to see the cracks in her composure.

“Status,” he said.

She didn’t look at him immediately.

“Alive,” she said.

The word carried weight.

“And we stay that way if we don’t do anything stupid.”

Ryan nodded once, eyes moving to the display.

The engine housing flickered in warning colors.

Sections isolated.

Others unstable.

He could see where she had cut the ship apart internally to keep it functioning.

Sacrifices.

Necessary ones.

“We’re not finishing the job,” she added.

Ryan’s jaw tightened.

“No,” he said.

The word came out flat.

Final.

Whatever claim he had been building out there had been broken the moment the missile hit.

“Then we leave,” she said.

Ryan exhaled slowly.

“Yeah.”

His eyes lingered on the external feed for a moment longer.

On the smoke.

On the damage.

On the cost.

“Ok,” Jennifer said, her voice shifting slightly, frustration bleeding through now that survival had stabilized. “We limp her back to port.”

Ryan let out a breath that might have been a laugh if it had any humor in it.

“Limp,” he repeated quietly.

“That’s optimistic.”

She glanced at him then, just briefly.

“Better than drifting.”

Ryan nodded.

She wasn’t wrong.

Again.

He leaned back slightly, one hand bracing against the console as he let the reality settle.

Barich.

The thought surfaced cleanly.

Cold.

“I can’t believe he took a shot at us,” Ryan said.

Jennifer's jaw tightened.

"What an absolute tool," she muttered.

Ryan shook his head once, more out of disbelief than disagreement.

There would be consequences.

Later.

If it came later.

He looked at the controls.

At the ship.

At the thin line between functioning and failure.

"Alright," he said, voice steady again. "Let's get her home."

A pause.

Then, quieter, almost as an afterthought:

"And after that, I'm taking a break."

Jennifer didn't respond.

But the corner of her mouth shifted just enough to acknowledge it.

Jennifer reached forward, hands settling onto the controls.

The ship trembled beneath him.

Alive.

Damaged.

But still moving.

CHAPTER FORTY-FOUR

SEDNA

The burn steadied into a rhythm Ryan could not control.

He felt it through the hull, through the deck beneath his boots, through the way the ship resisted every clean line of motion. Bessy no longer responded like a system under command. She reacted like something injured late, uneven, and unpredictable.

Jennifer's hands moved across the controls.

Precise.

Fast.

Unhesitating.

Ryan stood just behind her shoulder, watching the micro-corrections she fed into the ship, small bursts, trimmed vectors, and constant compensation for an engine that refused to behave consistently.

The damaged thruster flared again.

Too bright.

Then dimmed.

Jennifer adjusted before the imbalance could grow, countering the roll with a controlled input that settled the ship back onto a trajectory resembling stability.

Ryan let out a slow breath.

He trusted her.

That was the only reason this worked.

The spherical Sedna filled more of the viewport.

At first, it had been distant, abstract. Now it carried weight surface detail resolving into ridges and plains, long fractures cutting across ice-colored terrain like scars that had never healed.

Sedna.

Ryan felt the name settle into him.

“Back base Sedna,” he said quietly.

Jennifer didn’t look at him, but he saw the slight shift in her posture. She heard him.

“The most isolated place in the system.”

Bessy shuddered again.

Jennifer corrected instantly.

A short burst.

A counter-rotation.

Stability regained.

“A mixture of the very rich and the very poor,” Ryan continued. “Nothing in between.”

Jennifer exhaled through her nose.

“Sounds efficient,” she said.

Ryan almost smiled.

The planet grew larger.

The thin atmosphere caught the distant light, a faint glow that softened nothing. It only made the emptiness around it more obvious.

Jennifer and Ryan grew up together on Sedna.

Jennifer’s hands paused for a fraction of a second.

Then resumed.

“Sedna didn’t have much choice,” she said.

Ryan nodded.

“People don’t stay long,” he added. “Not unless they have to.”

“The ones that stay can’t leave,” she said.

Ryan watched the city emerge.

At first, just vertical lines breaking the horizon.

Then clearer.

Tall structures clustered together, rising from circular craters carved into the surface. Everything packed tight, as if distance itself was the enemy.

Isolation made physical.

“Sedna’s a gateway,” Ryan thought out loud. “Transit in and out of the system.”

Jennifer adjusted their descent profile, easing strain off the damaged engine.

“More like a choke point,” she said.

Ryan considered that.

Didn’t disagree.

“My parents are there,” he said after a moment.

Jennifer didn’t turn.

“Still?” she asked.

“Yeah.”

The word sat heavier than he expected.

Of all places.

The ship trembled again.

Stronger this time.

Jennifer compensated, tightening her inputs, smoothing out the instability before it could cascade.

Ryan watched her work.

The precision.

The control.

She wasn't just flying.

She was holding the ship together solely through motion.

"The city's built out of space concrete," Ryan said. "Thick. Heavy. Designed to keep the cold out and the heat in."

Jennifer glanced at the readouts.

"Let me guess."

Ryan exhaled.

"It doesn't do either very well."

She almost smiled.

The city filled the viewport now.

Grey.

Dense.

Uninviting.

A place designed to survive, not to live.

Ryan felt something settle in him.

Behind them, the wreck they had fought for was already gone from relevance.

Ahead, Sedna waited.

Jennifer leaned slightly into the controls, guiding Bessy down through an approach that left no margin for error.

Ryan relaxed beside her.

Watching.

And saying nothing.

Because there was nothing left to say that would change where they were going.

CHAPTER FORTY-FIVE

COLD WELCOME

The landing wasn't clean.

Ryan felt it through his knees before he heard it, a hard, uneven contact. Bessy's damaged landing assembly met the pad with more force than intended. The ship tilted slightly, compensators lagging just enough to make the motion uncomfortable rather than catastrophic.

Jennifer corrected instinctively.

Thrusters pulsed.

A brief hover.

Then a second, more controlled drop.

This time, the ship settled.

The engines wound down in staggered intervals, each one cutting out with a different tone. The cockpit display showed that even the ship itself was unsure whether it had survived the descent.

Ryan remained relaxed for a moment.

Listening.

Feeling.

Waiting for something else to fail.

Nothing did.

He exhaled.

“That’ll do,” Jennifer said, her voice dry, though the tension underneath it hadn’t gone anywhere.

Ryan nodded once, eyes drifting across the internal displays.

Damage reports still scrolled.

Still updating.

Still unresolved.

“Let’s not push her again today,” he said.

Jennifer let out a small, humorless breath.

“Wasn’t planning on it.”

Ryan turned toward the hatch.

The memory of the external damage sat sharply in his mind: the torn hull, the exposed systems, and the smoke that had followed them all the way down. Seeing it again, up close, grounded on a static surface, would make it real in a different way.

Permanent.

He opened the hatch.

Dry.

Thin.

The kind of cold that didn't bite at first but settled into the bones if you let it.

Sedna.

Ryan stepped out onto the pad.

The ground was solid.

Unforgiving.

The city rose beyond the perimeter walls, tall grey structures clustered tightly together, their surfaces worn by time and environment. Nothing here looked temporary.

Nothing looked welcoming.

Jennifer joined him a moment later, her movements slower now that the immediate pressure of survival had eased.

Ryan glanced back at Bessy.

The damage looked worse here.

Gravity made it heavier.

Real.

Sections sagged.

Scorch marks cut across the hull in jagged patterns.

Panels hung where they should have been sealed.

“She’s going to need more than patchwork,” Jennifer said quietly.

Ryan didn’t respond.

He already knew.

They moved through the access corridors toward the residential blocks.

The transition from landing pad to interior space was abrupt, metal giving way to thick, insulated walls that still failed to keep the cold out fully. The air inside was warmer, but not comfortable.

Functional.

Like everything else here.

Ryan knew the path without thinking.

Turns taken on instinct.

Distances measured by memory.

A long ride in an elevator.

Nothing had changed.

That was the problem.

They reached the door.

He paused for a fraction of a second.

Then opened it.

The room was small.

Contained.

Familiar in a way that felt distant.

A table sat in the center, solid and worn, surrounded by chairs that had seen too much use. The walls were made of the same thick, grey material as the rest of the city, lined with pipes and conduits that hummed faintly with the effort to maintain conditions close to livable.

His parents were already there.

Seated.

Waiting.

His father looked older than Ryan remembered.

Lines deeper.

Posture slightly heavier.

His mother watched him with a sharper expression, eyes moving immediately to the details of his suit, the wear, the fatigue.

Jennifer stepped in beside him.

The door closed behind them.

Sealing the room.

Sealing the moment.

Ryan took a seat.

The chair felt harder than it should.

Or maybe that was just him.

Silence settled across the table.

Then his father spoke.

“So let me get this right.”

The tone was calm.

Too calm.

“You took Bessy out to make money.”

A pause, “And brought her back damaged.”

Ryan didn’t answer immediately.

No version of this sounded better out loud.

Jennifer leaned forward slightly.

“It wasn’t Ryan’s fault,” she said. “Barich fired a missile.”

The words landed.

Heavy.

Ryan watched his father’s expression shift.

“A missile?” he asked.

Ryan nodded once.

“Yeah,” he said. “A missile.”

The simplicity of it made it worse.

His mother leaned back slightly, her expression tightening.

“Well,” she said, “that puts all of us in a bad position.”

Ryan didn’t look away.

"What a complete waste of space that Barich is."

There was no heat in her voice.

Just judgment.

Final.

His father shook his head slowly.

The motion carried more weight than any reaction.

"Well," he said, "you're going to have to go back to your former employer."

Ryan felt the stress slightly.

He already knew where this was going.

"Max," his father continued. "Owner of Sedna Spacecraft."

The name settled into the room.

Unwelcome.

Familiar.

"And ask for help," he finished. "Maybe even a job."

Ryan felt the resistance rise immediately.

Instinctive.

Strong.

He had left that behind.

For a reason.

But the reality sat in front of him.

Bessy.

Damaged.

Unusable without resources they did not have.

He glanced at Jennifer.

She didn't speak.

Didn't push.

But her expression was clear.

This wasn't optional.

Ryan looked back at his father.

Then down at the table.

Cold stone.

Solid.

Unmoving.

He exhaled slowly.

“Ok,” he said.

The word came out quieter than he intended.

Because on Sedna.

There weren’t many choices.

And the ones that existed were rarely good.

CHAPTER FORTY-SIX

TERMS OF RETURN

The workshop smelled like heat and metal that had never quite cooled.

Ryan felt it the moment he stepped inside, air thick with oil, insulation dust, and the faint ozone tang of circuitry pushed past safe tolerances. The space stretched wider than it first appeared, rows of benches and suspended rigs layered into depth, every surface occupied by parts in various states of usefulness.

Nothing here was decorative.

Everything was waiting to be used again.

He slowed without meaning to.

Jennifer walked just ahead of him, her pace steady, unbothered by the environment. She belonged here in a way Ryan never quite had. Where he saw weight, she saw systems. Where he felt history, she saw function.

Ryan's eyes moved across the room.

Tools.

Frames.

Half-built assemblies suspended from overhead rails.

Him.

Max stood near the center of the workshop, framed by light that filtered through high industrial panels. He held his helmet loosely at his side, posture relaxed, as if the space itself adjusted around him rather than the other way around.

Ryan stopped.

Max hadn't changed much.

Or maybe he had, just in ways that were harder to measure.

More settled.

More certain.

The kind of certainty that came from not having to leave.

Ryan became aware of his own stance.

The wear on his suit.

The damage he had just brought back with him.

Max smiled.

"Ryan. Jennifer."

His voice carried easily through the workshop, calm, controlled, already aware of more than he had said.

“I haven’t seen you in a long time.”

Ryan said nothing.

Max’s gaze moved over him.

“I heard,” he continued, almost casually, “you had trouble stepping outside your own spacecraft.”

The words landed lightly.

Too lightly.

Ryan felt the edge beneath them.

Intentional.

Ryan held his ground.

Didn’t react outwardly.

Inside, something tightened.

“That was one time,” he said.

The response came out flatter than he intended.

Defensivc, even if he hadn’t meant it to be.

Max’s expression didn’t change.

If anything, it settled.

"Of course," he said.

No judgment.

No agreement.

Just an acknowledgment that didn't commit to either.

Ryan's gaze shifted briefly across the workshop again.

Everywhere he looked, there was capacity.

Tools that could fix Bessy.

Systems that could rebuild what had been damaged.

Resources they did not have.

He felt it then.

The imbalance.

Clear.

Unavoidable.

Max had everything they needed.

And Max knew it.

Ryan brought his attention back to him.

Held it.

Said nothing.

Because whatever came next.

Would not be given freely.

CHAPTER FORTY-SEVEN

NO CREDIT

Max didn't move closer.

He didn't need to.

The workshop already belonged to him.

Ryan felt it in the room's spacing, in the way every tool had a place, in the quiet confidence of systems that worked because someone here understood them completely.

Max studied him.

"After last time," Max said, almost casually, "I'm not extending anything."

Jennifer shifted slightly beside Ryan.

Ryan held Max's gaze.

Didn't look away.

Because looking away would confirm it.

And he wasn't ready to give him that.

"You know this wasn't."

Max raised a hand.

Small movement.

Final.

“I know exactly what it was,” he said.

His voice didn’t rise.

It didn’t need to.

“A damaged ship. A missed opportunity. And you're coming back here because you don’t have another option.”

The words landed clean.

Too clean.

Ryan felt it.

The feeling that built slowly, quietly, controlled, inevitable.

“No job either,” Max added.

That one hit harder.

Ryan didn’t react outwardly.

But something inside him shifted.

That had been the fallback.

Unspoken.

But real.

Gone now.

Jennifer exhaled slowly.

“So what are you offering?” she asked.

Max’s attention flicked to her.

Then back to Ryan.

“Repair,” he said. “Full assessment. Parts. Labor.”

A pause.

Ryan waited.

Because there was always more.

Max smiled.

Small.

Precise.

“You pay upfront.”

Silence.

Ryan’s mind moved instantly.

Numbers.

Fuel.

Parts.

Distance.

There was no path.

Nothing.

Max already knew that.

Ryan exhaled slowly.

“Then why even say it?” he asked.

Max didn’t blink.

“Because that’s the price.”

Ryan felt the stress rising.

He nodded once.

Looked away.

Just for a second.

At the workshop.

At the tools.

At everything here that worked.

Then back.

"You know we can't pay that," he said.

Still controlled.

Max tilted his head slightly.

"Then you can't repair your ship."

Simple.

Complete.

Ryan nodded again.

Once.

Twice.

Like confirming a calculation.

He laughed.

Short.

Sharp.

Wrong.

Jennifer turned slightly toward him.

That hadn’t been part of the system.

Max didn’t react.

He just watched.

Ryan ran a hand across his face.

Exhaled.

And when he spoke.

The control wasn’t perfect anymore.

“You know what the worst part is?” he said.

Jennifer didn’t interrupt.

Max didn’t either.

Ryan took a step forward.

“You’re right,” he said. “Completely right.”

“I don’t have another option.”

The words hung there.

He let them.

Didn’t soften them.

Didn't redirect.

Max said nothing.

His voice wasn't louder.

But it carried something different now.

"You patch one thing, something else breaks. You stabilize that, something else starts slipping. You run the numbers, and they don't balance, but you go anyway because stopping isn't an option."

Jennifer's posture shifted.

Subtle.

Watching him now.

Ryan smirked.

"And then you get here," he said, gesturing lightly to the workshop, "and you realize the system doesn't care how hard you tried. Or how close you were. Or how many times you almost made it work."

"It just fails."

Silence.

Max studied him.

Differently now.

Ryan exhaled.

Slower.

The edge is fading slightly.

“So yeah,” he said. “You’re right. I don’t have another option.”

A pause.

Small.

But real.

Jennifer’s eyes flicked to Max.

Max didn’t move.

Didn’t speak.

Ryan held his gaze.

Didn’t look away this time.

“If we don’t fix Bessy,” Ryan said quietly, “we don’t go back out there.”

“No salvage. No parts. No work.”

The system unfolded.

“But if we do,” he continued, “we keep flying.”

Max's expression didn't change.

But his attention sharpened.

Ryan saw it.

Pressed.

"You don't extend credit," Ryan said. "Fine."

A breath.

"But you do business."

That hung there.

Max's fingers shifted slightly against the workbench.

The smallest movement.

But not nothing.

Ryan didn't push further.

Didn't overplay it.

He let the system sit between them.

Unresolved.

Max looked at him.

Longer this time.

A small exhale.

Almost a shift.

“You’re in a very bad position,” Max said.

Ryan nodded.

“Yeah.”

Max’s gaze flicked briefly to Jennifer.

Then back.

“And yet,” Max continued, “You’re still trying to negotiate.”

Ryan didn’t smile.

Didn’t pretend.

“Yeah,” he said again.

“Because stopping isn’t an option.”

Silence.

Different now.

Max straightened slightly.

Thinking.

Actually thinking.

“We’ll see,” he said.

CHAPTER FORTY-EIGHT

THE UNTHINKABLE

Max's smile didn't reach his eyes.

It lingered just long enough to feel intentional.

"What a terrible person that Barich is," he said, almost conversationally. "Imagine that."

Ryan said nothing.

Max leaned slightly on the workbench beside him, fingers resting near a disassembled actuator, as if the conversation and the machine were equally trivial to him.

"To tell you the truth," Max continued, lowering his voice just a fraction, "and I'll deny it if you repeat it."

He paused.

"A very long time ago, I couldn't get out of a spacecraft either."

Ryan's eyes narrowed slightly.

That was new.

Max straightened again.

"So," he finished lightly, "you have my sympathy."

Jennifer crossed her arms.

She didn't buy it.

Neither did Ryan.

Sympathy wasn't what Max dealt in.

"Then help us," Ryan said.

It came out more direct than he intended.

Less negotiation.

More demand.

Max's expression didn't change.

"What can I do, Max?" Ryan added, adjusting his tone, forcing it back under control. "I don't have that kind of money."

Max nodded slowly.

"I don't envy your position," he said.

And this time, for a brief moment.

It almost sounded true.

“You are going to have to do the unthinkable,” Max continued.

Ryan felt it before he heard it.

A shift.

A direction he didn’t want.

“And see your former partner.”

The words landed like an impact.

Ryan felt the stress.

“You mean,” he started, already knowing.

Max held his gaze.

“Yes.”

Ryan shook his head.

“No way.”

The response was immediate.

Instinctive.

Final.

“You mean that major mafia boss criminal Francis?” Ryan’s voice hardened. “No way.”

Jennifer glanced at him.

Max didn't react to the label.

He watched Ryan.

"No other way," Max said calmly.

Ryan exhaled sharply.

Turned slightly, pacing a single step before stopping himself.

This wasn't space.

He couldn't just move to think.

"And she just received a major payout from the courts," Max added.

That made Ryan stop completely.

Max let that sit.

"She has the money."

Silence followed.

Heavy.

Ryan stared at the floor for a moment.

Then back at Max.

Then away again.

His mind was already moving.

Paths.

Options.

Dead ends.

This one wasn't just difficult.

It was loaded.

History.

Complication.

Risk.

Jennifer spoke quietly.

"You said, former partner."

Ryan didn't answer.

Max did.

"They worked together," he said.

Ryan looked concerned.

"That's one way of putting it."

Max gave a small shrug.

"It's the only way that matters right now."

Ryan let out a slow breath.

Because Max was right.

That was the problem.

Emotion didn't change constraints.

And the constraint was clear.

No money.

No repair.

No ship.

No future.

Unless.

He closed his eyes briefly.

Saw it already.

The conversation.

The place.

Her.

Every version of it ended the same way.

Complicated.

Dangerous.

Personal.

He opened his eyes.

Looked at Max.

“You’re serious,” he said.

Max didn’t smile this time.

“Yes.”

Ryan nodded once.

Small.

Reluctant.

The decision wasn’t made.

But the direction was.

Jennifer watched him carefully.

“You don’t have to.”

“Yes,” Ryan said quietly.

He didn’t look at her.

He might hesitate.

“And I won’t like it,” he added.

Max leaned back slightly.

Satisfied.

Ryan turned toward the exit.

Each step is heavier than the last.

Because some doors.

Once reopened.

Didn’t close cleanly again.

CHAPTER FORTY-NINE

FRANCIS

The office was warmer than it should have been.

Soft lighting. Polished wood. Expensive silence.

Everything about it was designed to suggest comfort.

Everything about it was a lie.

Ryan stood just inside the doorway, unmoving.

Jennifer is beside him.

And on the desk.

Jennifer is in a projection.

Blue-white light rising from a circular emitter, forming a perfect, artificial version of Jennifer's body, clean, precise, dissected into glowing geometry.

A scan.

A statement.

A warning.

Ryan didn't look at it for long.

He looked at Francis.

She hadn't changed.

Not really.

Same posture.

Same stillness.

Same controlled presence that filled the room without effort.

Black dress. Sharp lines. Dark lips. That slight tilt of her head, like she was already halfway through a conclusion no one else had reached yet.

"Ryan and Jennifer," she said smoothly.

Her voice carried no surprise.

Only calculation.

"I wasn't expecting you."

That was a lie, too.

Ryan could tell.

She expected everything.

"You know," she continued, gesturing lightly toward the hologram, "many of these 'upgrades' Jennifer has appear to be illegal."

The word upgrades hung there.

Deliberate.

Clinical.

Dehumanizing.

Jennifer didn't react.

But Ryan felt the shift beside him.

Subtle.

Tension is tightening just beneath the surface.

"I could have you arrested just for that."

Francis smiled.

Ryan exhaled slowly.

He had prepared for this.

Standing in front of her again was different from planning it.

"You always did like opening with a threat," Ryan said.

Francis's eyes flicked to him.

Interest.

Brief.

"I always liked efficiency," she corrected.

Ryan stepped further into the room.

Deliberate.

No hesitation now.

"We're not here to argue about legality."

Francis raised an eyebrow slightly.

"No?"

"No."

Ryan glanced once at the hologram.

Then back to her.

"We need your help."

There it was.

Out.

Clean.

No negotiation dressing.

Francis studied him.

Assessing.

Comparing.

Measuring the distance between who he was.

And who he used to be.

“That,” she said softly, “is unexpected.”

Ryan almost smiled.

“Not really,” he said. “You always said I’d come back when I ran out of options.”

Francis’s lips curved slightly.

“That does sound like something I would say.”

Jennifer finally spoke.

Controlled.

Sharp.

“We don’t have time for this.”

Francis’s gaze shifted to her.

And stayed there longer than necessary.

Noticing.

Cataloguing.

Evaluating.

“You’ve improved,” Francis said.

It wasn’t a compliment.

It was an assessment.

Jennifer met her stare.

“I survive.”

A pause.

A flicker of something in Francis’s eyes.

Respect.

Or interest.

Or both.

“Clearly,” Francis said.

Ryan stepped in again.

Redirecting.

“We need funding,” he said. “Repairs. Fast.”

Francis didn’t look at him.

Still watching Jennifer.

“And why,” she asked, “would I invest in something already broken?”

Ryan didn’t answer immediately.

Because the answer wasn’t technical.

It wasn’t financial.

It was leverage.

And Francis didn’t deal in anything else.

“Because,” Ryan said finally, “you don’t invest in ships.”

Now she looked at him.

Fully.

“You invest in outcomes.”

Silence.

A slow smile.

Real this time.

Small.

Sharp.

Dangerous.

“There he is,” Francis said quietly.

Ryan didn’t move.

Didn’t react.

Didn’t give her anything.

This was the real conversation.

The one underneath everything else.

“What outcome,” Francis asked, “are you offering me?”

Ryan held her gaze.

And for a moment.

Everything else disappeared.

The room.

The hologram.

Jennifer.

Even the past.

All of it reduced to a single exchange.

Input.

Output.

Risk.

Return.

“We’re going back out,” Ryan said.

“Further than before.”

“And this time,” he added, “we’re not coming back empty.”

Francis leaned back slightly.

Considering.

Calculating.

Reconstructing the board.

New variables.

Old players.

“And you need me,” she said.

A statement.

“Yes.”

No hesitation.

No pride.

Just truth.

Francis’s smile deepened.

That was the currency she valued most.

Not power.

Leverage is built on necessity.

“Then,” she said softly, “We should discuss terms.”

Ryan felt it then.

The shift.

The moment the system locked in.

They weren’t asking anymore.

They were negotiating.

And that meant.

They were already in.

Behind him, the door slid shut.

Quiet.

Final.

Ryan knew that whatever this deal became, it would cost more than money.

CHAPTER FIFTY

THE COST

Francis did not answer immediately.

She turned instead.

Slowly.

Deliberately.

Toward the window.

The city stretched out behind her light, wealth, and motion. Towers rising like certainty.

Control, made visible.

“You should have called before,” she said quietly.

Ryan frowned.

“That’s what you just said,” he replied. “Why?”

Francis smiled again.

But this time.

There was something colder in it.

Because now.

She was about to explain.

“Because,” she said, turning back to face them, “you had something then.”

A pause.

Her eyes moved between Ryan and Jennifer.

Precise.

“Now,” she continued, “you have nothing.”

The words landed clean.

No exaggeration.

No insult.

Just assessment.

Ryan didn’t respond.

She wasn’t entirely wrong.

Bessy was damaged.

Their leverage is minimal.

Jennifer shifted slightly.

Always aware.

“So,” Francis continued, stepping closer, heels silent against the polished floor, “if I had funded you before.”

She stopped just short of them.

“I would have been buying into potential.”

Her gaze locked onto Ryan.

“Now,” she said, softer, sharper.

“I’m buying risk.”

Ryan met her eyes.

Didn’t flinch.

“Then price it,” he said.

That got her attention.

A flicker.

Approval.

Because that was the correct response.

Engagement.

Francis tilted her head slightly.

“You’ve learned,” she said.

Ryan didn’t smile.

“I’ve adapted.”

Then Francis stepped back.

Reclaiming space.

Reasserting control of the room.

“Very well,” she said.

She moved to her desk.

Tapped something unseen.

The hologram flickered.

Expanded.

Bessy appeared.

Damaged.

Exposed.

Broken lines of structure highlighted in cold blue geometry.

Impact vectors.

System failures.

Cost projections.

All of it, laid bare.

Jennifer’s eyes tracked it instantly.

Processing.

Calculating.

Ryan watched her, not the display.

Because of her reaction.

That mattered more.

She didn’t speak.

But he saw it.

The problem.

Bigger than they’d admitted.

Francis noticed too.

Of course she did.

“That,” Francis said, gesturing lightly, “is not a repair.”

She looked at Ryan.

"That is a rebuild."

Silence.

Heavy now.

Structural.

Ryan nodded once.

"Then we rebuild."

No hesitation.

Francis smiled again.

This time, genuine interest.

"And how," she asked, "do you propose to pay for that?"

Ryan stepped forward slightly.

Into the projection light.

Into the problem.

"By going further out," he said.

"Past the mapped salvage zones."

Jennifer turned her head toward him.

Sharp.

That hadn't been discussed.

Committed now.

"There's wreckage out there no one touches," he said. "Too far. Too risky."

He met Francis's gaze.

"That's where the value is."

Francis watched him.

Longer this time.

Actually listening.

"And you believe," she said slowly, "that you can reach it, with that?"

She gestured again to the broken image of Bessy.

Ryan didn't look back.

"Not like this," he said.

"That's why we're here."

Silence stretched.

Francis exhaled softly.

Decision forming.

"You're not asking for a loan," she said.

Ryan didn't reply.

Because she was right.

"You're asking for an investment," she continued.

Her eyes sharpened.

"And that means."

She stepped closer again.

"I set the terms."

Ryan nodded.

"Yes."

Jennifer spoke.

Quiet.

Controlled.

"What terms?"

Francis looked at her.

And smiled.

In a different way.

“You,” Francis said, “are part of the terms.”

The room shifted.

Instantly.

Ryan’s posture changed.

Subtle.

Protective.

Jennifer didn’t move.

But something in her eyes.

Locked.

Clarified.

“What does that mean?” Ryan asked.

Francis didn’t look at him.

Still watching Jennifer.

“It means,” Jennifer said, “I want access.”

A pause.

“To everything you are.”

Silence.

Jennifer held her gaze.

Unblinking.

“You already scanned me,” Jennifer said.

Francis tilted her head.

“That was a surface read.”

A faint smile.

“I’m talking about full integration.”

Ryan stepped forward.

“No.”

Immediate.

Flat.

Final.

Francis finally looked at him again.

And this time.

Her expression didn’t change.

“Then you don’t have a deal,” she said.

Just like that.

Clean.

Binary.

System closed.

Ryan felt it.

The edge.

The drop-off.

No negotiation space.

Unless he created it.

He glanced at Jennifer.

Just for a moment.

Jennifer looked back at him.

And in that look, there was no fear.

Only calculation.

Only awareness of cost.

Of trade.

Of consequence.

Then she looked back at Francis.

And spoke.

“Define integration.”

Ryan turned.

Surprised.

But Jennifer didn’t look at him.

Didn’t explain.

Didn’t soften it.

Because she was already inside the system.

Already negotiating.

Francis smiled.

Slow.

Satisfied.

“Now,” she said quietly.

“We’re talking.”

CHAPTER FIFTY-ONE

BREACH

The negotiation never finished.

It shattered.

Glass exploded inward.

Not from impact.

From pressure.

A concussive force ripped through the office, scattering paper, splintering wood, and tearing the moment apart before it could resolve.

Ryan turned.

Too late to process.

Just in time to see him.

Barich.

Standing in the doorway.

Bleeding.

Ragged.

Eyes burning with something beyond anger.

Something personal.

"You should've stayed out there," Barich snarled.

Then he opened fire.

The muzzle flash lit the room in violent bursts.

Rounds tore through everything: desk, wall, and air, turning space into a killing field.

Jennifer moved first.

Not thought.

No hesitation.

Execution.

She stepped into the line of fire.

Her arm snapped forward.

And light curved into existence.

A dense, precise blue shield formed in front of her.

The bullets hit.

And shattered.

Fragments ricocheted across the room.

Ryan stumbled back.

Barich adjusted instantly.

He wasn't reckless.

He was experienced.

He lowered his aim.

Compensated.

The next burst came tighter.

Smarter.

But not fast enough.

Ryan felt it.

Impact.

A brutal, internal punch.

He looked down.

Red.

Spreading.

Too fast.

Jennifer pivoted.

But the damage was already done.

Barich grinned.

A broken, satisfied expression.

“Missed you once,” he growled. “Not twice.”

He fired again.

Jennifer stepped forward.

Into the gunfire.

Holding the line.

Her stance locked.

Her system is adapting in real time.

She changed tactics.

Her free hand clenched.

Energy gathered.

Condensed.

Formed.

A blade of light.

Sharp.

Silent.

Decisive.

She moved.

Faster than Barich could react.

One step.

Through the storm of rounds.

Two.

Inside his range.

Barich tried to pivot.

Too late.

The blade cut clean.

Across the weapon.

Across him.

The gun split.

Barich staggered.

Shock replacing fury.

For a fraction of a second.

He looked at her.

Really looked.

Then he dropped.

The weapon clattered beside him.

Silence flooded the room.

Sudden.

Total.

Ryan collapsed.

Jennifer caught him before he hit the ground.

“Ryan.”

Her voice was steady.

But no longer neutral.

Pressure.

Stabilization.

Assessment.

The blood didn’t stop.

Behind them.

Francis stood still.

Watching.

Calculating again now.

But differently.

Because this wasn't leverage anymore.

This was an escalation.

Jennifer didn't look at her.

Didn't need to.

Flat.

Final.

Ryan tried to speak.

Nothing came out.

Jennifer lowered him carefully.

Her eyes lifted.

Focused.

Cold.

Directed now not at Barich.

Not in the room.

But at Francis.

Because this.

Was no longer negotiation.

This.

Was the consequence.

CHAPTER FIFTY-TWO

EXTRACTION

Jennifer did not hesitate.

She moved the moment Ryan dropped.

No discussion.

No permission.

No negotiation.

Action.

She seized him under the arms and pulled hard, dragging his weight across the shattered office floor, leaving a dark red trail behind them.

Ryan gasped.

A broken sound.

Francis shouted something.

Orders.

Security.

Control is trying to reassert itself.

But Jennifer didn't stop.

She didn't even look back.

Because priority had already shifted.

Primary objective: Ryan.

Everything else.

Irrelevant.

They hit the hallway.

Jennifer turned sharply, dragging him through the doorway just as armed footsteps thundered in the distance. Into the elevator, down into the street, then finally into a secluded alleyway.

Too slow.

All of them.

Always too slow.

Ryan's head rolled slightly.

His eyes struggled to focus.

"Jen."

Barely sound.

Barely there.

Jennifer dropped to one knee beside him.

Ryan's suit sprang into life. Scanning.

Blood loss estimation.

Trajectory mapping.

The suit healed the wound.

Ryan convulsed.

Pain cutting through the fading haze.

"Stay with me," she said.

Flat.

Controlled.

But beneath it.

Something else.

Something new.

Ryan tried to breathe.

Failed.

Tried again.

Air came in broken.

Wet.

Jennifer leaned closer.

Her optics flickered.

Internal overlays flood her vision.

The suit's damage assessment recalibrated in real time.

Critical.

Rapid decline.

Unacceptable.

The suit adjusted pressure.

Shifted angle.

Minimized flow.

"Listen," she said.

Closer now.

Focused entirely on him.

"You are not allowed to die."

Not a plea.

Not emotion.

Instruction.

Ryan almost laughed.

Almost.

Blood touched his lips.

"Wasn't… planning to…"

Jennifer ignored it.

Irrelevant.

Humor did not stabilize the hemorrhage.

Ryan's body jerked violently.

A sharp, raw scream tore out of him.

Then cut short.

Because of the pain.

Overrode everything.

Ryan's breathing stuttered.

Then caught.

Held.

Not failing.

Jennifer froze for half a second.

The suit.

Reassessing.

Recalculating.

Behind them.

Voices grew louder.

Closer.

Security.

Weapons.

Too late.

Still too late.

Alive.

Jennifer looked at him.

Really looked.

And for the first time.

There was no calculation.

Only confirmation.

Alive.

She stood.

Lifted him again.

Easier now.

Adjusted grip.

Rebalanced weight.

Then moved.

Faster.

Down the alleyway.

Out of the system.

Into the night.

Because whatever deal had existed.

Whatever negotiation had been forming.

Whatever control Francis thought she had.

Replaced by something else.

Something simpler.

Survival.

CHAPTER FIFTY-THREE

AFTERMATH

The world came back in fragments.

Light first.

Cold blue light, fractured across the inside of Ryan's visor.

Then sound.

Distant.

Muted.

Like the universe had been wrapped in cloth.

Then pain.

Sharp.

Immediate.

Real.

Ryan inhaled hard and regretted it instantly.

His chest burned.

Not the tearing, catastrophic pain from before.

Something else now.

Reconstructed.

Held together.

Temporary.

He blinked.

The alley resolved around him.

Wet pavement.

Overflowing bins.

Towering buildings above, their windows glowing like distant stars.

Jennifer.

Kneeling beside him.

Watching.

Not scanning.

Not calculating.

Watching.

"You're back," she said.

Simple.

Flat.

But there was something underneath it.

Something quieter.

Ryan shifted slightly, testing his body.

Bad idea.

Pain flared.

He didn't black out.

That was new.

"That sucked," he muttered.

Jennifer tilted her head.

"Your assessment is accurate."

Ryan let out a weak breath that almost became a laugh.

Almost.

He looked up.

And the HUD flickered across his vision.

MEDICAL STATUS: STABLE (CONDITIONAL)
TRAUMA: CHEST PENETRATION – PARTIAL REPAIR COMPLETE
NANOFIBRE SEAL: ACTIVE
STEM CELL INJECTION: IN PROGRESS
SUIT INTEGRITY: 63%
RECOMMENDATION: DO NOT MOVE

Ryan stared at it.

"Yeah, I'm definitely going to ignore that last part."

Jennifer didn't react.

Because she already knew.

"You were lucky," she said.

Ryan turned his head toward her.

She was close.

Closer than usual.

Not standing over him.

Not distant.

Present.

"What now?" she continued. "I really think your former partner genuinely hates you."

"You dumb nut."

Ryan winced.

Not from the injury this time.

"That's fair."

He looked past her.

Down the alley.

Dark.

Quiet.

Too quiet.

Barich was gone.

Or dead.

Ryan didn't know.

Didn't care.

Not right now.

Jennifer leaned in slightly.

Voice lower.

More focused.

“Next step.”

Ryan closed his eyes briefly.

Thinking.

Not about the fight.

Not about Francis.

Not about Barich.

The trap they were now inside.

Then he opened them again.

Clearer.

Decided.

“Let’s call Max.”

Jennifer studied him for a fraction of a second.

Then nodded.

Decision accepted.

She stood smoothly and offered a hand.

Ryan looked at it.

Then up at her.

Then, I took it.

Slowly.

Carefully.

Pain is still there.

But controlled.

Manageable.

Temporary.

He got to his feet.

Unsteady.

But standing.

Alive.

Above them.

The city moved on.

Unaware.

Uncaring.

Systems within systems.

Failures within failures.

And somewhere inside it.

Max.

Waiting.

Whether he knew it or not.

Ryan exhaled.

"Yeah," he said quietly. "Let's see how much trouble we're really in."

Jennifer didn't respond.

But she didn't need to.

Because now.

They were moving again.

CHAPTER FIFTY-FOUR

ESCALATION

The call connected before Ryan finished the motion.

The HUD snapped into clarity, replacing the alley with layered glass and light.

Max appeared clean, centered, and composed, as if chaos did not exist in his world.

Ryan blinked.

That alone was irritating.

"What?" Max said immediately. "She did what? Really?"

Ryan frowned.

"Yes," Max replied smoothly. "And I already don't like how this is going."

Jennifer crouched beside Ryan, her posture balanced, alert. Her gaze flicked between the HUD and the alley behind them, tracking threats that might no longer exist or might simply be waiting.

Ryan shifted, suppressing the pain.

"Barich opened fire. The office got torn apart. Jennifer engaged. I got," he hesitated, glancing at his HUD, "ventilated."

Max's expression didn't change.

But his eyes sharpened.

"I can see that."

A brief flicker passed across the HUD Max, pulling telemetry directly from Ryan's suit.

"Your biometrics are inventive," Max added.

"That's one word for it."

Max leaned slightly closer to his camera.

"Is Barich dead?"

Ryan exhaled.

"I don't know."

Jennifer answered instead.

"He is no longer a current threat."

Max nodded once.

Noted.

Filed.

Moved on.

“Well,” Max said, tone shifting, “there’s only one thing you can do now.”

Ryan already knew he wouldn’t like it.

Max didn’t pause.

“Call the big boss, John.”

Silence.

Even the alley seemed to hold its breath.

Ryan stared at the HUD.

“No.”

Max didn’t blink.

“That wasn’t a suggestion.”

Ryan shook his head slowly.

“You don’t escalate to him over this.”

Max’s expression hardened just slightly.

“You absolutely do.”

Jennifer tilted her head.

Max answered instantly.

“Barich was a problem.”

“John is the system that created the problem.”

Ryan looked away.

Max continued, voice calm, precise, surgical.

“You’ve now destroyed assets, triggered attention, and exposed upgraded tech that is, at best, legally questionable.”

Jennifer didn’t react.

Which, to Ryan, meant: confirmed.

Max’s eyes locked onto Ryan’s.

“You are no longer operating in a local failure.”

Ryan let that settle.

He knew this pattern.

He’d lived inside it before.

It never de-escalated on its own.

“What happens if we don’t call him?” Ryan asked.

Max didn’t hesitate.

“You become the problem instead of the exception.”

Jennifer looked at Ryan.

Decision point.

Ryan exhaled slowly.

Pain flared in his chest.

Real.

Immediate.

A reminder.

Everything had consequences.

“Alright,” Ryan said quietly.

Max nodded once.

Correct answer.

“I’ll send you the channel,” Max said. “Encrypted. One-time handshake. You get one shot at this.”

The HUD flickered, "new data stream incoming."

Ryan watched it form.

A doorway.

Or a trap.

Possibly both.

Max's voice softened just slightly.

"And Ryan?"

"Yeah."

"Try not to make this worse."

The connection is cut.

The alley returned.

Cold.

Wet.

Real.

Jennifer stood.

Ryan followed more slowly.

The new channel pulsed in his vision.

Waiting.

He looked at it.

Then at Jennifer.

Then back at it.

“Big boss,” he muttered.

Jennifer’s voice was steady.

“Yes.”

Ryan sighed.

“Yeah, this is going to go badly.”

But his hand still moved.

There was no opting out.

CHAPTER FIFTY-FIVE

TERMS OF POWER

The room was wrong.

That was Ryan's first thought.

Not luxurious.

Not impressive.

Wrong.

Everything in it was too deliberate.

The spacing of the furniture. The exact symmetry of the desk. The city framed perfectly behind the man.

Nothing accidental.

Nothing wasted.

Nothing uncontrolled.

Ryan didn't sit immediately.

Jennifer didn't move at all.

The man behind the desk watched them with quiet patience.

"Ryan, Jennifer, please sit," he said.

His voice was calm.

Not loud.

Not commanding.

Certain.

"I have been expecting you."

That landed harder than anything else.

Ryan slowly lowered himself into the chair.

Jennifer followed, precise and balanced, her posture alert but still.

The man folded his hands.

No introductions.

None needed.

This was John.

And John did not introduce himself.

"We have many things in common," John continued. "We both hate the mafia with a passion."

Ryan said nothing.

That wasn't a statement.

It was positioning.

"The organization I represent has a lot of resources," John went on. "Space elevators. Transportation. Infrastructure across many domains."

Ryan felt it immediately.

Scale.

Not criminal.

Not corporate.

Systemic.

"We would like to help you in your fight against Mr. Barich and the organization that Francis represents."

Help.

Ryan almost smiled.

Nothing at this level was helpful.

Only exchange.

Jennifer spoke first.

"One question. Why us?"

John looked at her.

Not dismissive.

Evaluating.

"Because you are already inside the problem," he said. "And because you survived it."

"That makes you useful."

Ryan leaned back slightly.

There it was.

Clean.

Honest.

Transactional.

"Ok," Ryan said. "Let's do this."

Jennifer glanced at him.

Not surprised.

Just confirming.

"Yes," she added.

Agreement locked.

John inclined his head slightly.

No approval.

Acknowledgment.

"Good," he said.

Then he leaned forward just a fraction.

And the room seemed to tighten around that movement.

"I only ask for one small favor in return."

Ryan didn't react.

But every system in his body did.

"There is a small ship in the outer regions that needs recovery," John continued. "If you agree to return the cargo to me, I will pay for the repair of your ship through Max."

Ryan's HUD flickered briefly.

Financial pathways.

Logistics.

Already aligning.

"And," John added, "I will ask my acquaintance Ming to outfit your ship with a number of weapons."

That changed things.

Significantly.

Jennifer spoke quietly.

"Define cargo."

John's eyes moved to her.

Careful.

"Contained," he said. "Intact. Non-negotiable."

Not an answer.

A boundary.

Ryan exhaled slowly.

There it was.

The real contract.

Unknown payload.

High-value recovery.

Implicit risk.

Guaranteed entanglement.

He looked at Jennifer.

She didn't nod.

Didn't shake her head.

But her eyes were sharp.

Calculating.

Then he looked back at John.

"You're not telling us what it is," Ryan said.

"No," John replied calmly.

"And if we open it?"

John held his gaze.

"Then you will have made a mistake."

Silence settled over the room.

Heavy.

Precise.

Ryan felt it click into place.

This wasn't a job.

It was onboarding.

He leaned forward slightly.

“Alright,” he said.

A pause.

“We’re in.”

Jennifer didn’t repeat it.

She didn’t need to.

She was already committed.

John leaned back.

Satisfied.

Not pleased.

Not relieved.

“Excellent,” he said.

Outside, the city continued to glow.

Inside, a new system had just accepted them.

CHAPTER FIFTY-SIX

MING'S SHOP

Not clean, sterile.

Burnt insulation.

Hot metal.

Improvised power.

Ryan paused just inside the doorway, letting his eyes adjust.

Weapons lined the walls.

Not displayed.

Stored.

Cataloged chaos.

Every surface carried something dangerous.

Rifles in partial assembly.
Power cells.
Barrels with heat scoring.
Things Ryan didn't immediately recognize, and that alone made them expensive.

Behind the counter, a man sat frozen.

Hands raised.

Eyes wide.

And pressed against his face, a gun.

The punk holding it grinned as if this were entertainment.

Not business.

Not survival.

Entertainment.

Ryan held a position.

Didn't rush.

Didn't speak immediately.

He observed.

Angle of the weapon.
Distance.
The punk's stance is loose, overconfident.
Finger tension is too eager.

Amateur.

Jennifer stood just behind him.

Still.

Watching.

Processing faster than him.

The man behind the counter, Ming, tried to speak.

“No help needed, I am with a customer,” he said, his voice tight and controlled.

Wrong tone.

Too fast.

Too sharp.

The punk shoved the gun harder into Ming’s cheek.

“Shut up and go away.”

Ryan tilted his head slightly.

Consider the room.

Considered the outcome.

“Well, that is not very nice.”

The punk glanced at him.

Annoyed.

Not threatened.

“Yeah?” the punk said. “What is an unarmed man going to do about it anyway?”

Ryan exhaled slowly.

He didn’t look at the gun.

Didn’t look at the punk.

Ryan looked at Ming.

Ryan smiled.

“Nothing,” Ryan said calmly.

Then he shifted his weight just enough.

“Because I have a Jennifer.”

The punk frowned.

Confused.

That was the moment.

Jennifer moved.

Not fast.

Precise.

Her arm extended a very long blade.

A clean, controlled line.

Blade deployment.

Silent.

Efficient.

The space between decision and consequence collapsed.

Ryan didn’t flinch.

Didn’t even step forward.

He already knew the outcome.

It was not improvisation.

This was system execution.

Behind the counter.

Ming froze even harder.

Then slowly, carefully.

He lowered his hands.

Still staring.

Still processing.

"No, stop, I am with a customer," he said again, voice shaking. "Please wait out the back of the store. Now, please."

Ryan stepped forward, finally.

Now that the variables were resolved.

Now that the system was stable.

He rested a hand lightly on the counter.

Casual.

Controlled.

"John sent us," he said.

That changed everything.

Ming's fear didn't disappear.

But it reorganized.

Shifted categories.

From an immediate threat.

Too dangerous an opportunity.

Ryan glanced briefly at Jennifer.

Then back to Ming.

CHAPTER FIFTY-SEVEN

SEESEE

The room was quieter than it should have been.

Too quiet for a place like this.

A workshop disguised as a kitchen.

Or a kitchen repurposed into something far more precise.

Metal surfaces.

Industrial fixtures.

Tools that didn't belong near food.

Ryan sat at the table, elbows resting lightly, posture controlled.

Watching.

Across from him.

It.

No.

Her.

She sat perfectly still.

Hands folded.

Head slightly tilted.

Painted porcelain over engineered precision.

Blue floral patterns traced across her synthetic skin like art pretending to be innocence.

She wore headphones.

Not decorative.

Integrated.

Functional.

Dangerous.

Jennifer leaned forward slightly.

Studying.

Calculating.

“Who is this?”

Ryan didn’t look away from the figure.

“This is SeeSee,” he said calmly.

A pause.

"Extremely illegal in nearly every way."

SeeSee's eyes shifted.

Not fully toward him.

Just enough.

Aware.

Ryan continued, voice even.

"Almost as illegal as your robot parts are."

Jennifer didn't react outwardly.

But Ryan knew her.

That landed.

He leaned back slightly.

Measured the room again.

Exit points.

Angles.

Distance to Jennifer.

Distance to SeeSee.

Probability trees branching quietly in his head.

He spoke, softer.

More direct.

“No, Jennifer, you are not going to fight her.”

That got a reaction.

A small one.

A smile.

Not warm.

Not amused.

Sharp.

“I think,” Jennifer said slowly, “I am going to have to.”

Ryan could feel the stress now.

He knew that tone.

Commitment threshold crossed.

Then she added.

Calm.

Certain.

"Once my sword is drawn, it has to draw blood."

Silence settled again.

But it had changed.

It was tension.

It was inevitable.

Ryan shifted his gaze back to SeeSee.

Looking for something.

A tell.

A delay.

An opening to prevent this from escalating.

Because if Jennifer was right.

Then this wasn't a conversation anymore.

It was a system collision.

And systems like these.

Didn't negotiate.

CHAPTER FIFTY-EIGHT

COLLISION

It happened faster than I thought.

Faster than hesitation.

Jennifer moved first.

Steel sang as her blade cleared its sheath clean, decisive, and inevitable.

SeeSee did not flinch.

Her arm rotated with mechanical precision, a hidden seam splitting open as a blade extended into her hand as it had always been there.

Two systems.

Two weapons.

Two conclusions.

They met in the center of the table.

Impact.

A crack like bone snapping, except it was metal.

The table split under the force.

Dust and splinters erupted upward, a shockwave rolling through the cramped room.

Ryan threw himself backward, arms up, instinct overriding analysis.

The world compressed into fragments.

Steel.

Motion.

Sound.

Jennifer pivoted, her strike flowing into a second arc, low and fast.

SeeSee caught it.

Not blocking.

Redirecting.

Her blade slid along Jennifer's edge, sparks spraying in a bright, violent line as the two weapons screamed against each other.

Jennifer stepped in.

Close.

Too close for a machine that calculated distance.

Her shoulder drove forward.

SeeSee's balance broke.

For a fraction of a second.

Enough.

Jennifer twisted.

And drove her blade down.

SeeSee hit the ground hard, the impact cracking tile beneath her.

But she was already moving.

Her arm snapped upward, blade intercepting Jennifer's downward strike.

Metal collided again.

Locked.

Tension.

Jennifer above.

See below.

Two opposing forces are grinding against each other.

Jennifer disengaged.

Explosive.

She launched upward, body compressing then releasing like a coiled spring.

Airborne.

Blade raised high.

Ryan saw it.

Trajectory.

Force.

Terminal intent.

“No!”

Too late.

Jennifer came down like a falling guillotine.

SeeSee rolled.

Not fast enough.

The blade struck the table instead.

Impact detonated the wood.

The entire structure flipped, splintering, fragments tearing through the air like shrapnel. SeeSee slid across the floor, recovering, and her movement's sharp but no longer perfect.

Damage.

Jennifer landed.

Controlled.

Already turning.

Already calculating the next strike. Ryan pressed himself against the wall, heart hammering.

He wasn't watching a fight.

He was watching escalation curves.

And they were vertical.

Because neither of them was hesitating.

Neither of them was negotiating.

This wasn't anger.

This wasn't emotion.

This was execution logic.

And the outcome was not going to be partial.

One of them was going to stop moving.

Ryan swallowed.

Mind racing.

Looking for interruption points.

Failure modes.

Anything.

Because if this continued.

There would be no system left to repair.

Only wreckage.

CHAPTER FIFTY-NINE

INTERRUPT

The strike landed.

Not clean.

Not elegant.

But final enough to matter.

Jennifer's blade drove down with terminal intent, yet the angle shifted at the last possible moment. Steel bit into SeeSee's forearm instead of her core.

A violent spray of fluid, dark, almost blood, but not splashed across the shattered table.

SeeSee's arm was severed.

The hand still clutched the sword.

For a fraction of a second, everything stopped.

Not physically.

Systemically.

SeeSee looked at the damage.

Not with pain.

With assessment.

Her remaining hand tightened on her weapon, but her posture changed just slightly.

A recalibration.

A reprioritization.

Jennifer stood over her, blade raised again, ready to complete the sequence.

Ryan saw it.

The next step.

The irreversible one.

"SeeSee, Jennifer, stop fighting."

Ming's voice cut through the room.

Not loud.

Not panicked.

Authoritative.

Precise.

It didn't interrupt the air.

It interrupted the logic.

Jennifer froze.

Not because she hesitated.

Because she processed.

SeeSee lowered her blade a fraction.

Her systems rerouted.

Damage protocols.

Threat reassessment.

Instruction override.

Ming stepped into the room, one hand raised, as if he were calming animals instead of machines capable of disassembly.

“Stop fighting immediately.”

The words landed like a command line.

Executed.

Jennifer’s blade lowered.

Not fully.

But enough.

Enough to prevent the next outcome.

“SeeSee, you have hurt yourself. Attend to it.”

SeeSee looked at her severed arm again.

Then at Jennifer.

Then back to the damage.

Priority stack reordered.

Self-repair.

She disengaged.

Not retreating.

Just exiting the conflict.

Ryan exhaled for the first time in what felt like minutes.

The room settled.

Dust drifting.

Fragments of the destroyed table are still shifting on the ground.

The silence after violence.

Ming turned to Ryan and Jennifer.

Calm.

Unbothered.

As if this were a minor inconvenience in a larger system.

"I will have to ask you to wait somewhere else while I retrofit your ship with weapons."

No apology.

No explanation.

Just process continuation.

Ryan blinked.

Looked at Jennifer.

Looked at the wreckage.

Looked at the blood-that-wasn't.

Then said the only thing that made sense in a universe that had clearly stopped making sense:

"Pub?"

Jennifer didn't hesitate.

"Pub."

CHAPTER SIXTY

THE LAST BOLT

The door slid open with a tired mechanical groan.

Light spilled out warm, amber, human.

A different world.

Ryan stepped in first.

Jennifer followed.

No one stopped them.

No one even really looked.

Because in a place like this, called *The Last Bolt,* you didn't stare at trouble.

You let it sit down and order a drink.

The air was thick.

Oil.

Alcohol.

Burnt circuits.

Voices layered over each other in a constant low hum: traders, mercs, mechanics, things that were once human, and things that had never been.

Ryan scanned the room automatically.

Exits.

Sightlines.

Threat clusters.

Then he stopped.

Because for the first time in a while.

Nothing was actively trying to kill him.

“That’s new,” he muttered.

Jennifer didn’t respond.

She was looking at the room differently.

Not tactically.

Structurally.

Weight-bearing beams.

Electrical routing.

Camera placements.

Patterns.

Always patterns.

They moved to a booth without speaking.

Sat.

Opposite each other.

A dented metal table between them.

A single hanging bulb above.

The kind of place where decisions happened quietly.

A mug hit the table.

Then another.

No one asked what they wanted.

Ryan stared at the drink.

Foam settling.

Hands still.

Then he looked up at Jennifer.

She was watching him.

Not like before.

Not calculating.

Not evaluating threat.

Just.

Watching.

“You almost killed her.”

Jennifer tilted her head slightly.

Correction processing.

“I did not,” she said calmly. “I stopped when instructed.”

“That wasn’t the plan.”

“That was not my plan either.”

Ryan exhaled slowly.

Ran a hand over his face.

“You escalated fast.”

Jennifer didn’t blink.

“She drew a weapon.”

“So did you.”

"She was hostile."

"So are you."

A pause.

Small.

But real.

Jennifer leaned forward slightly.

"Ryan," she said, her voice quieter now, "once my sword is drawn."

"I know," he cut in. "You made that very clear."

Silence settled between them.

Not uncomfortable.

Just loaded.

Around them, the bar continued as if nothing mattered.

Because here.

Nothing did.

Except for survival.

Ryan picked up his drink.

Took a slow sip.

Winced.

"Terrible."

Jennifer looked at her mug.

"Do I drink this?"

Ryan almost smiled.

"Up to you."

She considered it.

Actually considered it.

Then lifted the mug.

Paused.

"Is it harmful?"

"Probably."

She took a sip anyway.

No reaction.

A faint tilt of her head.

"Unpleasant," she concluded.

Ryan nodded.

"Yeah. That tracks."

Another pause.

Longer this time.

Ryan leaned back slightly.

Studied her.

Jennifer held his gaze.

No hesitation.

Ryan looked away.

Into the room.

At strangers who didn't care.

At lives that didn't intersect.

At a system that didn't pause.

Then back at her.

"Yeah," he said quietly. "That's the problem."

Jennifer didn't respond.

There wasn't a correct answer.

Only outcomes.

And consequences.

CHAPTER SIXTY-ONE

AN EXTRA PAIR OF HANDS

The foam on the drinks had just begun to settle when a shadow fell across the table.

Ryan didn't look up immediately.

He had already clocked the approach, heavy steps, confident, not trying to hide.

Not a threat.

But not harmless either.

Jennifer turned first.

Precise.

Curious.

Evaluating.

The man stood there in a worn exo-suit, helmet open, and grin wide enough to ignore the tension still hanging in the air from earlier.

Too wide.

Too easy.

"I heard you might be looking for help."

Ryan lifted his eyes.

Slow.

The man didn't sit.

Didn't ask.

Just stood there like he already belonged.

That alone was a signal.

Confidence or stupidity.

Sometimes the same thing.

Ryan leaned back slightly.

"People hear a lot of things."

The man laughed.

Open.

Unbothered.

"Yeah, but most of it's wrong. This one didn't sound wrong."

Jennifer was still watching him.

Not his face.

His hands.

His posture.

Balance.

Weight distribution.

Micro-adjustments.

She spoke before Ryan could.

“You approached without hesitation,” she said. “You assessed low immediate threat.”

The man blinked once.

Then smiled wider.

“Or I’m just friendly.”

“No,” Jennifer said. “You are not.”

Ryan almost smirked.

Almost.

“What do you want?” he asked.

“Name’s Liam,” the man said, finally pulling out a chair and sitting without permission. “I fly. Fix things. Get into places I probably shouldn’t. People say you’ve got issues with your ship.”

Ryan’s eyes narrowed slightly.

“That's so.”

“Yeah. Hard to get in. Hard to get out. Systems are a bit temperamental.”

Jennifer’s head tilted.

Slightly sharper this time.

“You have been discussing us,” she said.

“Not directly,” Liam replied easily. “Places like this? Information leaks. People talk.”

Ryan tapped his mug lightly against the table.

Thinking.

Not about the words.

About the angle.

Why him.

Why now.

“Why help?” Ryan asked.

Liam shrugged.

"Because I can. Because I'm good at what I do. And because ships like yours," he grinned again, "they don't come around often."

Jennifer leaned in slightly.

Interest increasing.

"You are motivated by challenge," she said.

"And money," Liam added.

"Honesty improves your probability of acceptance," Jennifer replied.

Ryan exhaled through his nose.

This was happening fast.

Too fast.

He glanced sideways at Jennifer.

That was the mistake.

Because she had already decided.

"You know what?" she said, turning back to Liam. "Yes. Welcome aboard, Liam."

Ryan blinked.

Once.

Then looked at her properly.

"That wasn't."

"He is useful," Jennifer said. "Your hesitation indicates uncertainty, not rejection."

Liam raised his mug.

"I like her."

Ryan didn't smile.

Didn't agree.

But he didn't say no either.

And that was enough.

Because somewhere underneath the instinct to reject.

There was a calculation forming.

More capability.

More risk.

More variables.

And maybe.

Exactly what they needed.

Ryan picked up his drink again.

Looked at Liam.

Then at Jennifer.

Then back to Liam.

“Alright,” he said finally. “You get one chance.”

Liam’s grin didn’t change.

Didn’t need to.

Because he’d already won the moment Jennifer spoke.

Ryan knew it.

Jennifer knew it.

That, more than anything, was the part Ryan disapproved of.

CHAPTER SIXTY-TWO

UNSTABLE SIGNAL

Ryan was still holding the mug when the world shifted.

Not physically.

Digitally.

A flicker barely perceptible ghosted across the inside of his helmet. Then the pub dissolved into layered transparency as the HUD forced itself forward.

A call.

Unscheduled.

Uninvited.

He didn't answer it.

Not immediately.

Jennifer noticed.

Of course she did.

"Your attention has shifted," she said calmly. "Incoming communication."

Ryan set the mug down.

Slow.

Deliberate.

“Yeah,” he muttered.

The interface pulsed again.

INCOMING TRANSMISSION UNSTABLE SIGNAL

That part he didn’t like.

Unstable meant distance.

Or interference.

Or someone who didn’t want to be tracked.

Ryan accepted.

The world collapsed into a tight frame of blue light and scanning lines. The pub dimmed into the background, muffled, irrelevant.

A face resolved.

Young.

Clean.

Too clean for the places Ryan usually dealt with.

“Max.”

Ryan didn’t say it as a question.

The man smiled slightly, like they’d spoken yesterday instead of… whenever it had last been.

“Your ship is now ready,” Max said.

No greeting.

No buildup.

Just business.

Ryan leaned back in his chair, eyes narrowing slightly.

“That was quick.”

“You will have to pick it up from the spaceport,” Max continued, ignoring the comment. “Given that you smashed up Ming’s place.”

Ryan exhaled.

Once.

Through his nose.

Behind him, Liam let out a low whistle.

"Yeah," Liam muttered, "I heard about that."

Jennifer didn't react.

Her attention was fixed on the projection.

Analyzing.

Cataloguing.

Max's image flickered slightly due to compression artifacts and signal degradation.

Not local.

Definitely not local.

Ryan leaned forward.

"Define 'ready.'"

A pause.

Fractional.

Max's eyes shifted not off-screen, but inward.

Processing.

"Operational," he said. "Upgraded. Within requested parameters."

"Within?" Ryan repeated.

That word mattered.

Max smiled again.

Same smile.

Didn't reach his eyes.

"You'll want to see it for yourself."

Ryan didn't like that answer.

Didn't like the phrasing.

Didn't like the fact that Max was controlling the conversation instead of responding to it.

Max's expression sharpened.

"Right," he said quietly. "Your ship is upgraded."

Ryan grimaced.

"Careful, public," Ryan said.

Max raised his hands slightly.

Not defensive.

Performative.

"Relax. You're not the only one who has been upgraded."

The signal flickered harder this time.

Static crawled across the edges of the display.

Time was running out.

Max's voice cut through it.

"Dock 17. Don't be late. Spaceport won't hold it indefinitely."

"Max," Ryan started.

But the feed was distorted.

Glitches.

Collapsed.

Gone.

Silence snapped back into place.

The pub returned in full.

Noise.

Heat.

Smell.

Reality.

Ryan stared at the space where the call had been.

Then leaned back slowly.

"Yeah," Liam said, grinning slightly. "That didn't sound ominous at all."

Jennifer tilted her head.

"Your discomfort is increasing."

Ryan stood.

Decision made.

"Drink's over."

Jennifer stood with him.

Immediate.

Liam hesitated.

Then followed.

Of course he did.

Ryan looked toward the exit.

Toward Dock 17.

Toward whatever Max had done to his ship.

“Let’s go see what Max meant.”

CHAPTER SIXTY-THREE

OUTSTANDING DEBTS

Ryan hadn't even taken three steps toward the exit before the HUD pulsed again.

Harder this time.

No instability warning.

No hesitation.

Just.

INCOMING TRANSMISSION

He stopped.

Closed his eyes briefly.

Exhaled.

"Busy day," Liam muttered behind him.

Jennifer didn't speak.

But she didn't need to.

Ryan accepted the call.

The world snapped back into blue light and layered data.

Her.

Francis.

Perfectly framed.

Perfectly composed.

Like she had been waiting.

“Ryan,” she said.

Not angry.

Not loud.

Controlled.

Which was worse?

“I heard you smashed up Ming’s place,” she continued. “After you smashed up my place.”

Ryan didn’t respond.

Not yet.

He already knew where this was going.

“I have told the cops,” she said.

There it was.

Direct.

Clean.

Weaponized.

“You'd better pay for it,” she added. “You better not be going off-world.”

Ryan’s jaw tightened slightly.

Behind him, Liam shifted.

Subtle.

Uncomfortable.

“You are in big trouble.”

Ryan tilted his head slightly.

Cold.

“You finished?” he asked.

Francis smiled.

Small.

Sharp.

"Oh, not even close."

Ryan cut her off.

Not aggressively.

Just decisively.

"Send the bill," he said. "I'll deal with it."

"That's not how this works," she replied.

"It is now."

Her eyes narrowed slightly.

She wasn't used to losing control of a conversation.

"You went to the cops," he said. "So go all the way. File it. Push it. Do whatever makes you feel better."

A pause.

Tiny.

But real.

Because that wasn't the response she expected.

Jennifer spoke.

Soft.

Precise.

“You are attempting to leverage,” she said to Francis. “However, your timing is inefficient.”

Francis’s eyes flicked to her.

Interest.

Annoyance.

Calculation.

“Give me a break, June?” Francis asked.

“Jennifer.”

Another pause.

Longer this time.

Francis smiled again.

Different.

“Oh,” she said quietly. “So that’s what you replaced me with.”

Ryan’s expression didn’t change.

Didn’t react.

Didn’t give her anything.

“That’s not what this is,” he said.

“No?” Francis tilted her head. “Because it looks like you upgraded.”

Jennifer didn’t respond.

Didn’t engage.

Which, somehow, made it worse.

Francis leaned slightly closer to the camera.

“Don’t leave,” she said softly. “You won’t get far.”

Ryan didn’t blink.

Didn’t hesitate.

“Watch me.”

And he cut the feed.

The HUD vanished.

Reality snapped back.

Noise.

Movement.

The exit ahead.

Liam let out a low breath.

"Okay," he said. "So we've got cops, angry exes, and a mystery ship upgrade."

Ryan started walking again.

"Yeah."

Jennifer fell into step beside him.

Perfect alignment.

"Your legal exposure has increased," she said.

Ryan glanced at her.

Dry.

"Thanks."

She looked back at him.

"I recommend leaving immediately."

Ryan gave a short nod.

"Already there."

Behind them.

The pub didn't matter anymore.

Ahead.

Dock 17 did.

And whatever waited there.

Was now a race.

CHAPTER SIXTY-FOUR

BESSY, ARMED AND DANGEROUS

Dock 17 was quieter than Ryan expected.

That was the first problem.

No mechanics.

No chatter.

No half-finished jobs scattered across the deck.

Just her.

Bessy sat in the center of the pad like something that had grown teeth while no one was looking.

Ryan stopped walking.

Liam didn't.

"Whoa," Liam breathed, stepping past him. "Okay, that's not what Max meant? That's."

"A war crime," Ryan finished quietly.

Because Bessy wasn't on the same ship.

Not even close.

Where there had once been patched plating and improvised repairs, there were now reinforced sections, integrated mounts, and clean weapon housings that looked like they had always belonged there.

They hadn't.

Ryan knew every scar on that ship.

Every shortcut.

Every compromise.

And now.

It was all.

Replaced.

Upgraded.

Weaponized.

Jennifer stepped forward.

Her gaze moved across the ship with machine precision.

"Structural integrity has increased," she said. "Weapon systems appear integrated, not appended."

Liam laughed.

"Yeah, no kidding. That's military-grade hardware."

His gaze was fixed on the display.

Didn't speak.

He was looking at the cockpit.

At the place he knew better than anywhere else.

And trying to figure out what Max had *really* done.

Inside, it was worse.

Cleaner.

Sharper.

Wrong.

Ryan sat in the pilot's seat slowly.

Like it might reject him.

It didn't.

The systems came alive instantly.

Too fast.

No lag.

No hesitation.

Jennifer slid into position beside him.

Liam took the rear station without asking.

Too comfortable.

Ryan noticed.

Filed it away.

“Power systems are optimal,” Jennifer said. “Navigation updated. Unknown subsystems detected.”

“There it is,” Ryan muttered. “Unknown.”

Liam leaned forward.

Grinning.

“You don’t look happy.”

Ryan didn’t look at him.

“Because I’m not.”

He ran his hand across the console.

Everything responded.

Everything worked.

That wasn’t the problem.

The problem was.

He didn't know *why*.

"Max doesn't do favors," Ryan said quietly.

Jennifer nodded.

"Agreed."

Liam shrugged.

"Or maybe he does, and you're just paranoid."

Ryan finally looked at him.

Flat.

"Stay that way," he said.

Liam's grin faded slightly.

Just slightly.

Launch clearance came faster than it should have.

That was the second problem.

No delays.

No questions.

No inspection.

Just.

CLEARED FOR DEPARTURE

Ryan didn't like that either.

"Yeah," Liam said, settling in. "This is definitely a setup."

Ryan powered up the engines.

"Probably."

Jennifer turned toward him.

"You are proceeding anyway."

"Yeah."

"Why?"

Ryan's eyes stayed forward.

Staying was worse.

Francis had already moved.

The cops would follow.

Whatever Max had done.

It was already done.

“We don’t get to sit still anymore,” he said.

Jennifer processed that.

Then nodded once.

“Understood.”

Bessy lifted.

Smooth.

Effortless.

Too effortless.

Ryan adjusted for resistance that wasn’t there.

Corrected for a drift that didn’t exist.

The ship responded like it knew what he wanted before he did.

That really wasn’t good.

They cleared the spaceport.

Atmosphere thinning.

Stars breaking through.

And then, full burn.

The engines roared.

Brighter.

Stronger.

Faster.

Bessy surged forward like it had been waiting for this.

Ryan gripped the controls.

Not fighting it.

But not trusting it either.

Beside him, Jennifer watched the data stream.

Behind him, Liam laughed.

“Okay,” Liam said, “I take it back. I love this ship.”

Ryan didn’t smile.

Didn’t relax.

Didn’t celebrate.

Because as the planet fell away behind them.

And the stars opened up ahead.

There was only one thought in his mind.

This wasn't an upgrade.

This was a move.

CHAPTER SIXTY-FIVE

COUNTERWEIGHT

The first thing Ryan noticed was the symmetry.

That was wrong.

Space wasn't supposed to look *balanced.*

It was supposed to be chaos drift, scatter, and debris moving like forgotten thoughts.

This was deliberate.

The structure hung in front of them like a decision someone had already made.

A massive counterweight, tethered by thick cables to a skeletal frame that curved out of view, its surface faceted and uneven, like an asteroid that had been organized.

Controlled.

Weaponized, maybe.

Ryan leaned forward slightly.

"Tell me that's not what I think it is."

Jennifer didn't answer immediately.

Her eyes moved, not scanning, not exactly *processing*.

“Density analysis complete,” she said.

A pause.

“That counterweight is approximately eighty-two percent gold and platinum.”

Liam let out a low whistle.

Then grinned.

“Pay day.”

Ryan didn’t answer right away.

He was still looking at it.

It wasn’t just valuable.

It was engineered.

Nobody leaves that much wealth floating in space without a reason.

“Or bait,” Ryan said quietly.

Liam shrugged.

“Everything’s bait. Just depends on whether you’re hungry.”

Ryan glanced at him.

There it was again.

Too comfortable.

Too ready.

Jennifer shifted slightly in her seat.

“Removal may cause structural consequences.”

“That’s a polite way of saying ‘don’t touch it,’” Ryan said.

“Yes.”

Liam leaned forward between them.

“Or a polite way of saying ‘jackpot with risk.’”

Ryan exhaled slowly.

Liam wasn’t wrong.

The ship drifted closer.

Bessy responded smoothly, adjusting vectors with that same unsettling precision.

No drift.

No resistance.

Like I *wanted* to approach.

Ryan didn't like that either.

"Hold position," he said.

The ship obeyed instantly.

Too instantly.

Jennifer's voice softened slightly.

Ryan's focus sharpened.

"Where?"

"Within the structure."

Liam's grin faded.

"Okay, now it's interesting."

Ryan nodded once.

Because now it wasn't just salvage.

Outside, the counterweight rotated slowly.

Cables flexed.

Tension adjusted in real time.

The whole structure breathed like something alive.

Ryan stared at it.

Then made the decision he always made.

The wrong one.

“We take a closer look.”

Liam smiled again.

Jennifer did not.

“Understood,” she said.

But there was a fraction of a pause before she said it.

And Ryan noticed.

Jennifer wasn’t just calculating risk.

She was anticipating the outcome.

Bessy moved.

Slow.

Controlled.

Closing the distance.

And as the structure grew larger in the viewport.

Ryan felt it.

That quiet, familiar certainty.

CHAPTER SIXTY-SIX

THE APPROACH

The structure appeared first as a distortion.

Not visible.

Resolvable.

Ryan adjusted his trajectory slightly, watching the star field rather than the object itself. The background didn't align. Points of light shifted out of expected positions, then returned, then shifted again.

Parallax inconsistency.

He slowed.

"Jennifer," he said. "Confirm forward object."

A delay.

Long enough to register.

"Unresolved mass detected," she replied. "Classification pending."

That wasn't useful.

Ryan reduced thrust further, letting inertia carry him closer. The distortion began to take form not as a silhouette but as a pattern that interrupted expectation. Lines that should have remained fixed bent around something that refused to present a stable edge.

“This isn’t debris,” he said.

“No,” Jennifer replied. “Preliminary structure detected.”

Ryan narrowed his focus.

The object resolved incrementally. Sections emerged, then disappeared, then reappeared in slightly different alignments: panels, framework, cavities; each element visible only long enough to contradict the last.

Not rotation.

Not drift.

Reconfiguration.

He adjusted his angle.

The structure changed.

Not in response.

Not delayed.

Just different.

Ryan stopped issuing corrections.

Let the drift continue.

“Distance,” Jennifer said.

“Not yet,” Ryan replied.

He needed a stable frame.

There wasn’t one.

The HUD attempted to map the object's building geometry, which collapsed as quickly as it formed. Planes intersected without joining. Depth values conflicted. Surfaces occupied multiple positions depending on the vector.

That shouldn’t happen.

Even fragmentation followed rules.

This didn’t.

Ryan moved closer, his boots clicking against the surface as he drew near.

The outer layer began to resolve into something that looked like damaged, torn plating, exposed internal structure, and deformation from impact.

He held that model for less than a second.

Then, I rejected it.

The lines didn't terminate.

They redirected.

"What hit this," Ryan said, "didn't break it."

"Clarify."

"It's still carrying a load."

A pause.

"Structure integrity appears compromised," Jennifer said.

Ryan shook his head slightly.

The word settled.

The HUD flickered.

Timing first.

Updates arriving just behind reality. Vector projections are adjusting late. Collision paths are corrected after movement instead of before.

Ryan noticed.

"Jennifer. Latency."

A pause.

“Within acceptable parameters.”

That was wrong.

Ryan introduced a small deviation that was controlled and measurable.

The correction came late.

Confirmed.

“Define acceptable.”

“Within operational thresholds.”

Not a number.

Ryan didn’t push it.

He was close now.

Too close for abstraction.

The structure filled his forward view, not as a single object but as layered inconsistencies. Surfaces folded into each other without intersection. Cavities opened, then sealed without transition. Edges that should have been sharp softened into curves that carried force instead of breaking it.

No failure points.

Only redirection.

Ryan extended his hand.

The HUD attempted to resolve the distance.

Failed.

Retried.

Returned conflicting values.

Closer.

Further.

Simultaneous.

He held position.

The numbers shifted again.

The model didn't stabilize.

His hand remained suspended.

The command was simple.

Advance.

He didn't move.

The path was clear.

The HUD confirmed it.

Vector stable. No collision.

Execution failed.

Ryan recalculated.

Same result.

Again.

Still correct.

Nothing wrong.

That was the problem.

“Ryan,” Jennifer said.

He didn’t respond.

Command and action had separated.

A fault condition.

“Ryan,” she repeated. “All systems nominal.”

The words didn’t fit the data.

He tried again.

Manual input.

Direct.

The command was entered.

No movement.

The structure shifted.

Not because of him.

Not after.

Just

Changed.

Angles compressed. Space redefined the surface he had been tracking, no longer aligned with his position.

The HUD tried to compensate.

Too late.

Ryan stopped issuing commands entirely.

The system was no longer reliable.

A second channel cut in.

“Ryan, you’re stalling.”

Liam.

Immediate. Close.

Ryan didn't look away.

"Latency," he said.

"Then stop using it," Liam replied. "Move."

Ryan didn't move.

The structure shifted again.

Closer.

Not through motion.

Through redefinition.

Distance collapsed without traversal.

"Ryan," Liam said, sharper now, "you wait, you drift."

No response.

"You drift, you're gone."

Statement of outcome.

No emphasis.

Ryan's breathing echoed in the helmet. Not fast. Not slow.

Out of sequence.

The full model wouldn’t resolve.

Too many variables.

Too many contradictions.

“Forget the model,” Liam said. “One movement.”

Ryan’s eyes flicked to the HUD.

Then away.

It couldn’t help.

“Just the next step,” Liam said.

That changed the problem.

Not solvable.

Reduced.

Ryan exhaled once.

Interrupting the loop.

His hand released the frame.

He moved.

Late.

Imprecise.

Forward.

The structure shifted.

Not reacting.

Not responding.

Existing differently.

The path he had committed to no longer existed.

Collision warning spiked.

Ryan fired thrusters.

Correction lagged.

He overshot.

Corrected again.

Still misaligned.

"This thing is not static," he said.

"Negative," Jennifer replied immediately. "No external actuation detected."

"Then explain the shift."

A pause.

Longer.

"Unknown."

Ryan forced distance.

Thrusters firing harder now.

The structure resisted.

Not physically.

Perceptually.

Distance increased, but proximity didn't resolve.

As if separation required more than motion.

Release.

Abrupt.

The HUD stabilized.

Vectors snapped back into alignment.

Distance resolved.

Ryan drifted back, breathing controlled again, gaze fixed on the structure.

It held.

Unchanged.

Or appearing to.

“Status,” he said.

A brief pause.

“All systems nominal,” Jennifer replied.

Ryan watched the structure.

Then said, quietly:

“That’s not true.”

CHAPTER SIXTY-SEVEN

CROSSING THE LINE

Ryan steadied himself on the hull.

The metal vibrated faintly beneath his boots, not movement, not quite, but a low, constant hum that hadn't been there before.

Or maybe he had only just noticed it.

"Jennifer," he said, "confirm any field effects around the structure?"

A pause.

Too long.

"Ryan… readings are inconsistent."

He didn't like that.

"Define inconsistent."

"Spatial drift without vector."

Ryan exhaled slowly.

That wasn't a thing.

Liam crouched beside him, gloved hand pressed to the surface of the smaller ship they had reached, a sleek, abandoned-looking craft tethered loosely within the counterweight's influence.

"This one's dead," Liam said. "No power. No lights."

"Then why is it still holding position?" Ryan asked.

Liam didn't answer.

Because there wasn't a good answer.

The tether line from Bessy stretched behind them, gently curving, not straight, not slack, but wrong in a way Ryan couldn't quite define.

Like it wasn't obeying simple physics anymore.

He forced his focus forward.

"Entry point?" he asked.

Liam pointed.

"There. Forward hatch. Looks manual."

Ryan nodded.

"Stay clipped. No drifting."

They moved together across the hull of the derelict ship, boots locking in rhythm. The surface was colder than Bessy. Older. Untouched.

Or abandoned.

Ryan reached the hatch.

Ran a gloved hand over the seam.

No markings.

No insignia.

Nothing to tell him who had built it or why they had left it here.

“Pressure?” he asked.

“Internal atmosphere unknown,” Jennifer replied. “No detectable leakage.”

“So it’s sealed.”

“Yes.”

Ryan hesitated.

Then gripped the manual release.

“On three,” he said.

Liam braced beside him.

“One.”

Ryan felt his pulse in his fingertips.

“Two.”

The hum beneath them deepened.

“Three.”

He pulled.

The hatch resisted.

Then gave.

Not explosively.

Not violently.

Just opened.

Slowly.

Smoothly.

As if something on the other side had been waiting.

Darkness inside.

Not empty.

Just unlit.

Ryan angled his helmet light forward.

The beam cut through the dust.

No.

Not dust.

Particles.

Suspended.

Not drifting.

Held.

Just like the debris outside.

Liam leaned in.

“Creepy,” he muttered.

Ryan didn’t respond.

Because the particles weren’t random.

They were arranged.

Subtle.

But deliberate.

Patterns.

“Jennifer,” Ryan said quietly, “I need you to record everything.”

“I already am.”

Good.

Because this wasn’t salvageable anymore.

Ryan placed one boot inside.

Then the other.

The transition was immediate.

The hum vanished.

The sense of direction up, down, and forward collapsed into something softer.

Uncertain.

He grabbed the hatch frame instinctively.

“Gravity?” Liam asked.

“Not stable,” Jennifer said. “Localized field variations.”

Ryan swallowed.

“Stay close.”

Behind them, the open hatch remained.

Framed against the stars.

Against Bessy.

Against everything that still made sense.

Inside, the ship breathed.

Not air.

Not sound.

But structure.

Alive in a way Ryan couldn't define.

"Ryan," Jennifer said.

Her voice was different now.

Filtered.

Distant.

"Your signal is degrading."

Ryan looked back at the hatch.

It already felt further away.

"Copy," he said.

Then turned forward.

“Alright,” he said quietly.

“We’re inside.”

CHAPTER SIXTY-EIGHT

THE STILL BODY

Ryan saw it before his mind could process it.

A shape.

Human.

Wrong.

It hung just beyond the forward console, framed by the stars caught in the ship's internal field like everything else here.

Suspended.

Perfectly still.

"Liam," Ryan's voice dropped. "Do you see that?"

"Yeah."

No humor this time.

No confidence.

They moved closer.

Slow.

Careful.

As if speed might disturb whatever invisible system held the body in place.

The suit was old.

Not ancient but not recent either.

Surface scoring microfractures along the joints. Dust embedded in the seams seems to have been drifting for a long time before being stopped.

Ryan reached out.

Stopped himself.

“Jennifer, scan.”

Silence.

Then static.

“Signal degraded, attempting reconstruction.”

Ryan felt a wave of stress.

“Just tell me if he’s alive.”

Another pause.

“No biological activity detected.”

Dead.

Liam circled slightly, tether line trailing in a lazy curve that didn't behave like a tether should.

"Helmet integrity's compromised," he said quietly.

Ryan followed his gaze.

There are fine cracks across the visor.

Dark staining inside.

Dried.

Old.

"Not poison," Liam added. "More like decompression trauma. But."

"But what?"

Liam shook his head slowly.

"He didn't drift."

Ryan looked again.

The body wasn't floating away.

Wasn't rotating.

Wasn't responding to any micro-movement at all.

It was fixed.

Like a specimen pinned in space.

Ryan's nerves returned.

"Max?"

The name slipped out before he could stop it.

Because of the suit.

The build.

The configuration.

No.

"That makes no sense," Ryan said, louder now. "Max was just, he just."

His thoughts fractured.

Time didn't line up.

Cause didn't line up.

Nothing lined up.

"Ryan," Liam said carefully, "we don't know it's him."

Ryan stared at the body.

At the posture.

At the hand, slightly curled as if reaching for something that never came.

“I don’t understand,” Ryan said.

And he meant it.

Not confusion.

Not uncertainty.

A fundamental break.

“Liam,” Ryan’s voice tightened. “I think this might be a trap.”

The ship answered.

Not with sound.

With movement.

The particles in the air shifted.

Subtly.

Rearranging.

The body moved.

Just a fraction.

Not drifting.

Not falling.

Turning.

Ryan froze.

“Did you see?”

“I saw it.”

The helmet.

The cracked visor.

The dead man’s face.

Tilted.

Toward them.

And somewhere, deep in the structure of the ship.

Something woke up.

CHAPTER SIXTY-NINE

WEAPONS HOT

The warning hit before Ryan understood the words.

Jennifer's voice cut across the channel, stripped of its usual precision.

"Barich inbound. Weapons active."

Ryan turned toward the hatch, too fast, his boots scraping against a surface that no longer held still. The interior geometry had shifted again. Not enough to see, to feel. Angles misaligned by degrees, his body registered before his eyes could confirm.

"Say again," he said, but the request had already lost relevance.

Time had collapsed.

He pushed through the hatch into open space. Outside, orientation returned immediately. Black, absolute, unambiguous. No false frames. No shifting references. Just vectors and distance.

"Liam. We're leaving."

Silence.

Ryan's gaze snapped to Liam's last position.

Empty.

His mind rejected it instantly.

Incorrect reference. Misaligned viewpoint.

He adjusted his position, rotated slightly, and recalculated the line of sight.

There.

Too far out.

The tether was angled incorrectly, with tension inconsistent with both vectors. It trembled, transmitting a pattern Ryan didn't want to resolve.

"Liam."

Not a command now.

Verification.

Liam turned, slow inside the helmet. The movement lagged, as if the signal had degraded across distance.

Ryan registered details with unwanted clarity.

There is a slight asymmetry in Liam's stance. The way he held readiness was like a baseline condition, the habit of moving early, deciding fast.

He had once said, half-joking, that hesitation killed faster than a vacuum.

“With you,” Liam said. “Just.”

The first strike cut him off.

Light arrived as a force.

A line of white carved across the derelict behind Liam, not illuminating but erasing, slicing through the structure without resistance. The shock transmitted through Ryan’s suit was a deep mechanical vibration that bypassed thought and went straight to instinct.

Ryan flinched, one arm rising uselessly.

“Move,” Jennifer said.

Ryan fired thrusters, vectoring toward Liam before the HUD could resolve a path. Warnings flooded his vision: conflicts, projections, predicted failure states, but they lagged behind his movement.

The second strike aligned perfectly.

Ryan saw it.

Origin.

Trajectory.

Intersection.

For a fraction of a second, the system was complete.

Then it broke.

The beam passed through Liam.

No explosion.

No debris.

No thermal bloom.

Just absence.

The space where Liam had been collapsed into nothing, the line continuing forward unchanged, as if no interaction had occurred.

Ryan's HUD tried to compensate.

Distance markers flickered.

Target lock failed, reacquired, failed again.

Vector prediction returned null.

That wasn't possible.

The mass could not be set to zero without a transition.

There had to be an intermediate state. Fragmentation. Dispersion. Signal decay.

Something.

The system required continuity.

“No,” Ryan said, but the word had no anchor.

The tether went slack.

Not snapping. Not recoiling.

Just losing purpose.

It drifted, a curve without tension, no longer describing a relationship between two points.

Ryan reached for it.

His hand closed late, passing through the space where it had been a second earlier. His timing was off. Not slow, misaligned.

He corrected.

Overcorrected.

The HUD stuttered again, feeding him vectors that didn’t match his motion.

“Ryan,” Jennifer said. “You are being targeted. Move.”

The instruction parsed.

Execution did not follow.

Ryan's gaze locked onto the empty coordinates, searching for residuals. Heat signature. Particulate scatter. Signal noise.

Nothing.

Clean.

Too clean.

A third strike tore across the hull, closer now. The impact forced a response, his suit compensating, thrusters firing hard, pushing him off-axis.

Movement returned before comprehension did.

He collided with the hatch, one hand catching the edge, momentum carrying him inside as the structure shifted again under external stress.

"Ryan, respond."

No response.

Because the response required a stable model, and he had just failed.

He pulled himself through, dragging the tether behind him. It snagged briefly, then slipped free, following him into the interior like a loose variable no longer bound to anything.

Inside, the ship behaved differently.

Not just damaged.

Reactive.

Structures shifted out of phase with applied force, delayed in ways that suggested internal processes Ryan couldn't map. Particles in the air drifted against the expected flow. Surfaces flexed, then held, then flexed again.

Ryan barely registered it.

His focus kept returning to the same point.

The last known position.

The exact coordinates where Liam had been.

His breathing came fast, uneven, fogging the inside of his visor.

There should have been a remainder.

All failures leave artifacts.

This left none.

"Ryan," Jennifer said, quieter now. Controlled. "Move to extraction. Now."

Extraction.

Defined path.

Input output.

Survivable state.

Ryan understood the sequence.

He couldn't trust it.

"Ryan."

No escalation. No explanation.

Just his name.

That was enough.

Not to fix the system.

But to bypass it.

Ryan closed his eyes for a fraction of a second, interrupting the loop, severing the recursive replay of the same impossible event.

When he opened them, the HUD stabilized.

Not correct.

But usable.

Vectors returned.

Warnings aligned.

Exit path resolved.

The system still functioned.

Even if part of it no longer existed.

He moved.

Not because it made sense.

Because staying meant aligning with the next strike.

Behind him, another beam carved through the ship, flooding the interior with hard white light through fresh fractures.

Ryan did not turn.

There was nothing left to verify.

CHAPTER SEVENTY

RETURN FIRE

Jennifer didn't react immediately.

For a fraction of a second, she did nothing.

Ryan's scream still echoed through the channel raw, distorted, and unresolved. It lingered in the system like a signal without termination.

Liam was gone.

The confirmation sat there.

Absolute.

No recovery path.

No alternative interpretation.

The system closed.

Jennifer inhaled once.

Slow.

Controlled.

Then she moved.

Her hands dropped to the console, not with panic or force, but with precision, inputs followed in rapid sequence, each deliberate and narrowing the problem.

Target acquisition.
Thermal isolation.
Vector prediction.

Barich's ship cut across the display, already repositioning. Fast. Aggressive. Confident.

Assuming advantage.

That was his mistake.

Jennifer filtered the noise.

Removed Ryan's channel from primary audio. Not muted, never ignored, but deprioritized. There would be time for that later.

Now there was only the system.

"Alright," she said quietly, voice flat, stripped of everything unnecessary. "Let's solve this."

Bessy responded instantly.

Not because it understood.

Because it was designed to obey.

Weapon systems unfolded across the interface rail assemblies extending along the hull, missile bays cycling open, capacitors charging in controlled sequence.

Energy draw spiked.

Jennifer rerouted.

Life support dipped by two percent.

Acceptable.

She overlaid predictive models across Barich's trajectory.

Not where he was.

Where he would be.

Three seconds. Five. Eight.

He was flying aggressively, cutting vectors, minimizing travel time, and accepting instability for speed.

That gave her an opening.

"Got you," she said.

Not emotional.

Mathematical.

She locked the solution.

“Fire.”

The first rail discharge cut across the void not as chaos, but as a line. Clean. Precise. Timed against predicted movement rather than observed position.

Barich reacted.

Too late.

The round struck along his forward arc, not a direct hit but enough to force correction. His vector shifted slightly but remained measurable.

Jennifer adjusted instantly.

Second solution.

Missiles were deployed not as a spread, but as a constraint. They didn’t aim to hit.

They aimed to remove options.

Barich’s ship accelerated, trying to break the envelope.

Exactly as predicted.

“Now.”

The beam fired.

Not continuous.

Not wasteful.

A controlled burst, aligned with the only remaining viable path.

It connected.

This time, clean.

The impact wasn't dramatic.

Not at first.

A flare.

A breach.

Then cascading failure.

Heat signatures spiked across the hull as internal systems lost containment. Structural integrity dropped in sharp, measurable steps.

Barich tried to compensate.

Thrusters fired erratically.

Too late.

Jennifer watched it unfold without moving.

Not reacting.

Tracking.

The explosion built from within, pressure and heat feeding into failure until the structure could no longer contain it.

Release.

The ship ruptured.

Fragments pushed outward in expanding vectors, each one predictable, and each one already accounted for in her system.

Jennifer adjusted Bessy's orientation slightly, shielding critical surfaces from debris.

Minimal movement.

Maximum effect.

Silence returned.

Not complete.

But close enough.

No escape pods.

No secondary signals.

No movement.

Barich dead.

Jennifer kept her hands on the console a moment longer.

Not because she needed to.

Because the system hadn't fully settled yet.

Then, slowly, she leaned back.

Exhaled.

Once.

Controlled.

And only then did she restore Ryan's channel to full.

CHAPTER SEVENTY-ONE

THE TOWER

Ryan sat in silence.

The hum of the station wrapped around him low, constant, indifferent.

Across the small table, Jennifer watched him carefully, her expression softer now, the sharp edge from battle replaced with something quieter. Almost human.

"I can't believe Liam is dead," Ryan said, his voice heavy, distant. "We only just met."

He stared into the glass in his hand but didn't drink.

"And Max, poor Max."

The words felt inadequate. Small. Meaningless against the scale of it.

Jennifer reached across the table, placing her hand over his.

The contact was deliberate.

Grounding.

"Someone set this up," she said. "This wasn't random."

Ryan looked up slowly.

Her green eyes held his.

“It has to be John,” she continued. “The old one. The one who sent you out here. He knew about the gold. He knew about the ship. And now Max is dead.”

Ryan exhaled, long and controlled, but it didn’t steady him.

“No,” he said. “It doesn’t make sense.”

But even as he said it, the system-builder part of his mind was already assembling the pieces.

Too many coincidences.

Too clean.

Too aligned.

A setup.

Ryan leaned back, eyes drifting past Jennifer to the viewport beyond the station walls.

Rising from the barren planet below.

The tower.

It pierced the sky like a blade.

Impossible in scale.

A single, monolithic structure anchored into the planet's crust, its surface alive with faint lines of light that pulsed upward toward a glowing apex.

A signal.

Or a warning.

"That's where he is," Jennifer said quietly.

Ryan didn't respond immediately.

He studied it.

Engineer first.

Always.

The base structure suggested something older than the surrounding installations, foundational rather than decorative. Energy conduits ran vertically, converging at the top. Not a communications array.

Power.

Massive power.

"Yeah," Ryan said finally.

His voice had changed.

Colder now.

Focused.

“We go there.”

Jennifer smiled slightly.

“Thought you’d say that.”

Ryan stood.

Grief is still there.

But contained.

Filed away.

Converted into something usable.

“And we’re taking that gold counterweight,” he added.

Jennifer’s smile widened.

“Obviously.”

Outside, the tower pulsed again.

A slow, deliberate rhythm.

As if it knew they were coming

CHAPTER SEVENTY-TWO

THE ARGUMENT

The room was quiet.

Too quiet.

Ryan stood opposite John, the city glowing behind him like a grid of cold stars. The old man sat perfectly still, hands resting on the desk, as if nothing had happened, as if people hadn't died.

"You are back," John said calmly. "I did not expect your return."

Ryan didn't sit.

"Why did you do it?" he asked. His voice was controlled, but only just. "Why did you kill Max?"

John's expression didn't change.

A slight pause.

"Please understand," he said, "someone else made me a very persuasive argument."

Jennifer stepped forward slightly.

"I thought you hated Barich?"

John’s eyes flicked to her.

“I do. He slept with the woman I love.”

That made it worse.

Ryan’s mind turned fast now.

Not random.

Not revenge.

Not profit alone.

Pressure.

Leverage.

A system forcing outcomes.

“Who?” Ryan asked.

But John didn’t answer.

The door slid open.

Soft.

Deliberate.

Ryan turned.

And immediately wished he hadn’t.

Francis.

She stood framed in the doorway, composed, smiling, as if she had just walked into a dinner party instead of the center of a disaster.

“Hello, Ryan,” she said lightly.

Jennifer groaned. “Oh no, not this girl again.”

Ryan didn’t speak.

Didn’t move.

Francis stepped inside.

Every movement is controlled.

Intentional.

“I think there’s been some confusion,” she said.

Ryan let out a short, disbelieving laugh.

“Confusion?”

She stopped a few steps from them.

Close enough now.

Too close.

“Yes,” she said. “For example.”

She tilted her head slightly.

“I slept with him.”

Silence.

Ryan blinked.

“What?”

She continued, almost conversational.

“I slept with Max. With Liam. Even Ming.”

Jennifer covered her mouth.

Ryan stared at her, trying to process it, failing.

“I slept with all your friends.”

The words didn’t land all at once.

They spread.

Like contamination.

“Oh my god, why?” Ryan said.

Not angry.

Just lost.

Francis smiled.

Not kindly.

Jennifer shook her head slowly, “This is insane.”

Francis turned to her.

“Oh, Jennifer,” she said. “I think you’ve met SeeSee before.”

Jennifer froze.

Francis’s smile widened.

“She’s had some upgrades.”

The room changed.

Not physically.

But the feeling of it.

Like something hidden had just been named.

Ryan felt it then.

The pattern.

The manipulation.

The way events had been nudged.

Not chaos.

Design.

He looked at John.

Then at Francis.

“You’re not the top of this,” he said quietly.

Not a question.

Francis didn’t answer.

But her smile said enough.

Something bigger was moving.

And they were already inside it.

CHAPTER SEVENTY-THREE

UPGRADES

It happened too fast.

One second, Jennifer was standing.

The next impact.

SeeSee hit her like a weapon.

The wall behind Jennifer exploded outward in a spray of dust and shattered composite as her body slammed through it, metal screaming under force.

Ryan didn't even register moving.

"JENNIFER"

SeeSee followed through the breach.

Fluid.

Precise.

Predatory.

They hit the ground together in a tangle of limbs and metal, but there was no struggle, only dominance.

SeeSee on top.

Always on top.

Her hand locked around Jennifer's throat.

Fingers tightening.

Servos whining.

Jennifer's systems spiked.

Warning lights flared across her vision.

Pressure thresholds exceeded.

Structural integrity compromised.

"Upgrade complete," SeeSee said softly.

Jennifer tried to move.

Couldn't.

SeeSee leaned closer.

Her face was calm.

Cold.

Perfect.

A slight tilt of her head.

Almost curious.

Ryan staggered forward, but stopped.

Because he saw it.

The difference.

This wasn't just strength.

It was coordination.

Latency near zero.

Predictive movement.

Every micro-adjustment is pre-calculated.

A closed-loop system.

Self-optimizing.

Jennifer's fingers twitched.

Fought.

SeeSee noticed.

Of course she did.

She adjusted pressure by a fraction.

Enough.

Jennifer's movement stopped instantly.

Ryan’s mind raced.

Not emotion.

Not panic.

Analysis.

“She’s not just stronger,” he said quietly.

“She’s running ahead of you.”

SeeSee’s eyes flicked toward him.

Recognition.

“Correct,” she said.

Jennifer forced out a strained sound.

“Ryan, don’t analyze.”

That broke it.

Ryan moved.

He grabbed a broken section of metal from the wall and swung.

Hard.

SeeSee released Jennifer.

Not because of the strike.

Because she had already calculated it.

She shifted.

Minimal.

Efficient.

The metal bar missed her head by millimeters.

She caught Ryan’s wrist mid-swing.

Stopped it.

Completely.

The force should have carried through.

Didn’t.

She held him there.

Like physics didn’t apply.

Crushed.

Ryan dropped to one knee, gasping, pain flaring up his arm.

SeeSee looked between them.

Evaluating.

“Two variables,” she said.

“Neither optimal.”

Jennifer lay against the rubble, systems struggling to reboot.

Ryan forced himself up, shaking.

Across the room.

Francis watched.

Smiling.

John didn’t move.

Ryan looked at Jennifer.

Then back at SeeSee.

He understood the real problem.

“You’re not the weapon,” he said.

SeeSee paused.

Just slightly.

Ryan’s eyes shifted to Francis.

"She is."

Francis smiled wider.

And outside.

Far beyond the shattered wall.

The tower pulsed again.

Brighter this time.

CHAPTER SEVENTY-FOUR

THE LOGIC OF FEAR

The tower burned cold light into the sky.

It wasn't just a structure.

It was a signal.

A statement.

Ryan stood at the viewport, the curve of the observation ring framing the alien horizon like a wound in space.

The world below was dead stone and frozen silence.

Francis stood opposite him.

Perfect posture.

Perfect control.

As if nothing in the universe could touch her.

Ryan broke first.

"Why did you sleep with all my friends?"

The words hung there.

Small.

Human.

Fragile.

Francis didn't laugh.

Didn't flinch.

She answered like it was obvious.

"Because love is weak."

Ryan's jaw tightened.

But he didn't interrupt.

"You are a coward," she continued, her voice calm, almost gentle. "You survive by fear. You build your world around it. You call that safety."

She stepped closer.

Controlled.

"Your fear keeps you alive."

A pause.

A shift.

"But I don't get that luxury."

Ryan’s eyes flicked to the tower.

Then back to her.

“I have to be strong,” she said. “All the time.”

“I have to remove weakness.”

Another step closer.

Now she was within arm’s reach.

Ryan let the moment pass without acting.

“I can’t afford love.”

Her eyes locked onto his.

“I have to kill everything I love.”

Silence.

Ryan felt it then.

Not anger.

Not betrayal.

Clarity.

“You’re not strong,” he said quietly.

Francis tilted her head.

Curious.

That landed.

Not visibly.

But something shifted.

Ryan gestured toward the tower.

Francis's expression hardened.

Just slightly.

"I chose this."

Ryan shook his head.

"No."

He stepped forward.

Closing the distance.

A breath.

"That's not strength."

He looked straight into her eyes.

For a moment.

Just a moment.

Something flickered behind her expression.

“You analyze everything,” Francis said softly. “That’s your weakness.”

Ryan almost smiled.

“No,” he said.

Outside.

Brighter.

Closer.

CHAPTER SEVENTY-FIVE

ELIMINATION

Jennifer stood beside SeeSee at the observation ring, both framed by the vast circular window. The dead world stretched beneath them, the tower rising like a needle through bone.

For a moment.

They were still.

Two machines.

Two reflections.

SeeSee turned her head slightly.

Studying Jennifer.

Curious.

Jennifer didn't answer immediately.

Her eyes flicked to the tower.

Then back.

"So did you," she started.

A pause.

SeeSee stepped closer.

Jennifer smiled faintly.

“You always try to kill me.”

SeeSee’s lips curved.

Almost amusement.

Jennifer’s eyes hardened.

“It never is with you.”

Soft.

Patient.

A tilt of her head.

“Those are inefficiencies.”

Jennifer stepped forward.

Now they were close.

Too close.

SeeSee’s eyes flickered.

Processing.

Jennifer didn’t look away.

"Only if you're afraid of them."

That word again.

Fear.

SeeSee moved.

Fast.

Her hand shot out.

Gripping Jennifer's wrist.

The glass behind them creaked.

Jennifer twisted.

Breaking the hold.

But SeeSee was already moving again.

A strike.

A counter.

Metal against metal.

Precision.

Speed.

Neither held back.

The window fractured.

Hairline cracks are spreading across the observation ring.

Outside.

The tower.

Jennifer blocked.

Turned.

Shoved.

"Yes," she said.

The word hit harder than the blow.

SeeSee paused.

Just a fraction.

"That is your failure."

The crack became a break.

Glass exploded inward.

Then outward.

Pressure is tearing reality apart in a single violent instant.

Everything went silent.

Vacuum.

Fragments of crystal spun into space.

SeeSee lost footing.

Her body pulled toward the void.

Jennifer moved.

Not to strike.

To grab.

Her hand locked around SeeSee's wrist.

For a moment.

They hung there.

Between inside and nothing.

SeeSee looked at her.

Confusion.

Real.

Jennifer strained.

Holding her.

Fighting the pull.

“I’m not you.”

Another crack.

The frame gave way.

Jennifer made a decision.

Not logical.

Human.

She pushed.

SeeSee’s eyes widened.

Not fear.

Something else.

Then she was gone.

Spinning into the cold.

Silent.

Endless.

Jennifer slammed against the inner frame.

Caught herself.

Pulled back inside as emergency shutters screamed closed.

Brighter than ever.

Jennifer looked out through the fractured viewport.

At the falling shape.

At the tower.

She understood.

This wasn’t about strength.

CHAPTER SEVENTY-SIX

SYSTEM LIMIT

The room was quiet.

Resolved.

Ryan did not move.

There was no version of this that changed with motion.

Francis watched Jennifer.

Only Jennifer.

“Begin,” Francis said.

Jennifer did not respond.

Not immediately.

Her gaze held.

Tracking.

“What are you doing?” Ryan asked.

Francis smiled.

“You see?” she said.

"No," Ryan said. "You don't."

Jennifer stepped forward.

Not toward Ryan.

Toward Francis.

Francis tilted her head.

"There isn't."

A pause.

Jennifer nodded.

"For a moment," Francis started to say.

Ryan exhaled.

That was the error.

Jennifer stepped closer.

Within reach.

"Define 'moment,'" Jennifer said.

Silence.

"Understood," Jennifer said.

She reached out.

Took Francis's wrist.

No force.

No hesitation.

Francis didn't react.

Not yet.

"You don't have control here," she said.

Jennifer tilted her head.

Her grip tightened.

Francis's expression shifted.

Slightly.

Jennifer shook her head.

Small.

Final.

"No," she said. Ryan moved.

Stopped.

"Jennifer."

Ryan understood.

Too late to matter.

Francis pulled back.

“You don’t get to choose this.”

A step closer.

Francis’s eyes widened.

That was enough.

Ryan felt the edge of it.

“Jennifer,” he said, “What are you doing?”

She moved.

Final.

Francis vanished.

No sound.

No recovery.

Ryan didn’t look.

Silence.

Jennifer released her grip.

Stepped back.

Still.

Then Jennifer turned to him.

Ryan stared at her.

A pause.

Ryan exhaled.

That was the change.

“Okay,” he said.

Jennifer studied him.

Ryan looked out.

Into systems that didn’t care.

Then back.

“We keep flying?”

Jennifer nodded.

This time, different.

John didn’t wait. Clean. Predictable.

SeeSee’s signal dropped on later searches after the fall.

No trace.

The End.

If you like this book, please read the other titles by the same author via Amazon KDP.

Tanks on a Spaceship

https://www.amazon.com/dp/B0GRG6B496

Intergalactic Junkyard

https://www.amazon.com/dp/B0GSF9DML2

How to Date and Other Teenage Fantasies

https://www.amazon.com/dp/B0GTTTP1J8

The Note Singer

https://www.amazon.com/dp/B0GX2YLXQY

Any review would be greatly appreciated.

www.ingramcontent.com/pod-product-compliance
Lightning Source LLC
LaVergne TN
LVHW012337100826
845148LV00018B/2703

* 9 7 8 1 7 6 4 6 2 2 7 3 8 *